THE ENTERTAINING BOOK

Teresa

and

Auberon Waugh

·

THE

ENTERTAINING

BOOK

·

Illustrated by

Glynn Boyd Harte

·

Hamish
Hamilton

London

First published in Great Britain 1986
by Hamish Hamilton Ltd
27 Wrights Lane London W8 5TZ

Copyright © 1986 by Teresa and Auberon Waugh
Illustrations copyright © 1986 by Glynn Boyd Harte

Book design by Gerald Cinamon

British Library Cataloguing in Publication Data

Waugh, Teresa
The entertaining book.
1. Entertaining
I. Title   II. Waugh, Auberon   III. Boyd
Harte, Glynn
642′.4   TX731
ISBN 0-241-11936-7

Typeset by MS Filmsetting Ltd, Frome, Somerset
Printed and bound in Spain
by Cayfosa Industria Gráfica, Barcelona

Introduction
by
Teresa Waugh

Anyone with a copy of *Mrs Beeton's Household Management*, the complete works of Elizabeth David and a little imagination, can become an excellent cook. There is absolutely no need for anything else. And yet more and more is written about food and cooking every year.

In the years after the war my mother was in the vanguard of the good food movement. Guests to our house always knew that they would have delicious food, and French friends casually remarked that it was all right staying with the Onslows "*parcequ'on bouffe comme chez soi*". It is true that during those years my mother employed a cook, but never a trained cook, always an inexperienced girl whom she could train in her own way, and so my mother herself spent many hours in the kitchen.

As a result of this I was always aware of good food. I remember people at school boasting about how their mothers made the best chocolate mousse or the best trifle and I never argued, but arrogantly kept to myself the absolute truth that my mother was a better cook than any of theirs.

But now times have changed and almost anyone that any of us knows is a pretty good cook. I can think of one or two friends whose cooking is outstanding. These people have a flair and a delicacy all of their own as well as patience and a dedication to detail. So it is quite unusual nowadays to be invited out to dinner and to have nasty food. Gone are the days of thick tasteless soup followed by chicken in white sauce and watery vegetables followed by tinned fruit salad. Gone are the walloping great potatoes and the pale beige, gelatinous chocolate mousse of which my school friends were so proud. Gone the salad cream and vinegary beetroot. Gone for ever the over-cooked, powdery beef, the lifeless stewed fruit and the tapioca pudding.

5

My children's generation has been brought up on a mixture of Camembert, junk food and avocado pears – such things would have been unheard of in a post-war nursery.

So now we are all, one way or another, committed to good food. It is no longer *mal vu* to discuss what you are eating or to congratulate your hostess on the dinner she has served. Practically no one has a cook, practically everyone is committed to food to a greater or lesser extent, and in addition vast numbers of women who go to work are desparately seeking new ways of feeding a hungry family quickly and well. Reading about food becomes a way of picking another person's brains.

Someone else may be able to provide a new twist to a *blanquette de veau* or they may merely jog your memory and remind you of the possibility of a dandelion salad.

I lay no claim to being an original cook. Everything I have learned I have learned from, among others, my mother, Elizabeth David, Mrs Beeton and from years of living on and off in France.

There are times when one grows so bored with one's own food that one can hardly bear to contemplate the meals that lie ahead like so many murky rivers to be crossed. Even the well-thumbed pages of Elizabeth David's *French Country Cooking* seem unable to tempt the jaded appetite. One stares aimlessly through the butcher's shop window. Bloody joints of meat appear grotesque, chicken is pale and insipid – there is nothing new. At the greengrocer's the tomatoes have a bold, cold look about them. The avocado pears are unripe and life is barely worth living.

One way to escape from this appalling state of *ennui*, which, it must be remembered, is deeply hurtful to one's family, is to dine with friends where an unexpected taste of caraway seed in the courgettes, an hollandaise sauce, a home-made cake or even an especially delicious salad will remind one that there is more to life than toasted cheese. Then the gloom will begin to fade and life in the kitchen will once again seem rosy. If, on the other hand, no one invites you out during this time, then renewed inspiration must be sought from the printed word and perhaps this is one of the reasons why there are so many printed words on the subject.

We all long for a new approach, a new slant, perhaps just a kind word from someone whose prejudices coincide with our own will able to help revive our interest, to whet the appetite and to send us hurrying back to the stove.

One of the disadvantages of the gastronomic revolution which has taken place since the war is that, to a certain extent, things have become too easily available.

Avocado pears used to be a treat, but now they are, if anything, overused. Fresh pasta is available in every shop in every beastly shopping precinct from Aberdeen to Brindisi; strawberries are around in January and red kidney beans come in tins. The search for something unusual or even faintly surprising has become increasingly difficult as *mange tout* and French beans come daintily packed by Marks & Spencer. We have become embarrassingly spoiled, and yet for all that we must go on eating and feeding our families and friends.

Perhaps what we really need now is not an endless supply of new ingredients but just a fresh approach to the old ones. We do not need more mangoes, more *mange tout* and more ladies's fingers in order to eat well. As I write I have only to cast my mind back to the dinner served to me last night by a French friend. Her tenderloin of pork was accompanied by a dish of sliced roast sweet apples, and how delicious and simple they were.

I can only hope that, in the pages which follow, the greedy but exhausted cook may find more ideas of this kind to revive his flagging spirits and to encourage him back to the kitchen.

Wine Introduction
by
Auberon Waugh

It may be true to say that the days of rotten cooking are "gone forever" now that middle-class housewives do their own cooking, although I think I would dispute it. Many middle-class households seem to have given up on meals altogether. Mothers have jobs, or have found some other means of fulfilling themselves. Other members of the family are left to help themselves from the fridge at whatever time they choose, to whatever food they find there: eaten alone, without conversation or anything to drink, except possibly milk. Then everybody gets on with the important things of life: watching television or videos, playing with the home computer or pursuing some dismal school project for homework.

But if one forgets the new or upwardly concentrates on the traditional upper middle and professional families who would, as recently as thirty years ago, have expected to employ a cook, then it is undoubtedly true that cooking has improved and that, where meals are still served, there is a commitment to good food. I wish I could say the same about wine.

Although wine consumption in Britain has advanced in leaps and bounds doubling in the past four years, the vastly greater part of this increase has been at the bottom end of the market, in sugared-up Deutsche Tafelwein and Euro-blends. These are served in pubs and unpretentious restaurants by the glass. One would like to think that they represent the nursery slopes of wine-drinking, and that people will go on to serious wines, or at any rate better ones, but the truth is that these beverages are a taste in themselves, belonging more to the Babycham tradition – derived from pears – than anything previously seen from the grape. Since the so-called "dry" whites in this price range are even nastier, there is little hope this corner of the market will ever make the leap into serious wine drinking.

However, the real threat does not come from these wines, which are beginning to usurp beer in our unisex age as the main drink of the video generation. The real threat comes from a strange tradition which has grown up among the wine-drinking classes for serving the cheapest possible wine. Neither Deutsche Tafelwein nor the Euro-blends nor even their older sisters, the Liebfraumilchs, have ever made much of an appearance on middle-class dining tables, but it is a sad and strange fact that hosts who would never stint on the gin, whisky or vodka, and who would certainly never buy inferior meat or vegetables because they were a little bit cheaper, actually *boast* of the cheapness of their wines, and will travel all over town to buy a bottle which is 10p. or 15p. cheaper. They say they prefer plonk, but what they are drinking is not plonk in the traditional sense – rough country wine, often with the sour and earthy tastes of rotting beechwood which some people undoubtedly enjoy. They are drinking mass-produced, heavily pasteurised wines, the better ones with very little taste at all, the worse ones with a marked taste of chemicals.

One reason for this may be that people are aware of a whole range of knowledge of wine which they do not possess and have not the time to acquire. They are irritated by the pretentiousness of wine snobs and wine bores. It is an area in which they are not prepared to compete. Rather than take even the minimum amount of trouble to try several of the wines available at their local super-market in the price range they can afford and decide which they like best, they go for the cheapest, and defiantly expect their guests to agree that it is not too bad.

One does not need to be a wine snob or a wine bore to see that this attitude very much reduces a person's chances of enjoying one of the greatest pleasures of life. With a little extra effort, and a little extra money – perhaps as little as 30p. or 50p. a bottle – they will be glimpsing the delights available to them. There are some people, much richer than myself, who groan at the thought of spending an extra 30p. or 50p. on a bottle of wine. In no other field would a sum like 30p. or 50p. assume the slightest importance. When pricing a dinner party for eight, it makes no more than £4 difference – about the cost of an unwanted and unnecessary extra glass of gin or sherry all round. The difference in the enjoyment of the meal can be enormous. Yet people insist on skimping in this one field.

Another reason may be the effort involved. Table wine is quite unlike video equipment, or motor cars, or even vintage port and brandy, where the more money you spend the better will be the result. It is possible to spend vast sums of money on a bottle of wine – a reputable claret from a reputable dealer – and find it quite undrinkable. Occasionally, this is because it belongs to a bad year, but far more often because it is too young. Almost the whole wine trade is concerned to push its wine out as fast as it can, years before it is ready to drink. Older vintages have become scarce and expensive. Fewer and fewer people nowadays have the facilities for storing wine, or the

patience to start a wine cellar from scratch. For instance the much-vaunted 1982 vintage in Bordeaux will not be ready to drink at all, where the better wines are concerned, for another ten years, and will not be approaching its peak, in most cases, for fifteen years. Yet they are being sold for between £60 and £80 a bottle for the *premiers crus* – Lafite, Latour, Mouton-Rothschild, Château Margaux, etc. – and over £40 a bottle for the more prestigious *deuxième crus* – Pichon-Longueville, Contesse de Lalande, Léoville-Las Cases, etc. Anybody who buys them and drinks them now, thinking he is giving himself a treat, will suffer a terrible disappointment. They are quite disgusting. The same is true of the 1983 Burgundies and the sturdy red wines from the northern Rhône – Hermitage, Côte Rôtie, Cornas – which enjoyed a similar *annus mirabilis* in 1983. In fact, to a greater or lesser extent, it is true over the whole red wine scene dominated by the classic red grapes of Cabernet, Pinot Noir and Syrah: that, the more expensive the wine in your department store or wine merchant, the nastier it will taste.

The result of all this is to spoil the market in fine wines and discredit everything which serious wine writers say about the subject. Many wine merchants have no Burgundy older than 1976 on their lists – some of the minor 1976 Burgundies are just coming up for drinking now, but the grander ones need several years – and no Bordeaux older than 1978. In fact, few of the 1970s have come round yet. Snobbery undoubtedly adds to the pleasures of wine, but snobbery can take one only so far. Those 1978s may be wonderful wines in another three to eight years, but by the time a person has opened his third or fourth Château Lafite at £55 the bottle (twice or three times that sum if he is drinking it in a restaurant) and found himself drinking something which is thin, hard and sharp – infinitely less appealing than the 1983 red Côtes du Rhône from Sainsbury's at £2.80 the bottle – he will begin to lose his enthusiasm for the fine claret idea.

My plea that people should spend more money on their wines is therefore heavily qualified. An even more important thing is to put more effort into choosing wines you like. There are some perfectly decent wines in the very cheapest price brackets, some outstandingly good ones in the next two (at present around £2.80–£4.99) and some brilliant, unforgettable wines in the more expensive areas, if only people can make the effort to discover what they like most and chase it. I am in the happy and privileged position of running the *Spectator* Wine Club, which enables me to taste most of the wines on the market and present my discoveries to readers of the *Spectator* magazine once a month, like a good dog laying a bone at its master's feet. If, in the course of adding some wine notes to my wife's declarations on the even more important subject of food, I can persuade a few people to choose their wines more carefully, I feel that I have added something significant to the sum of human happiness and my spell on earth will not have been entirely wasted. For further reading. I recommend Hugh Johnson's *Pocket Wine Book*, published annually by Mitchell Beazely at around £5. It contains more information for its size than anyone would have thought possible, and is possibly the best book ever written on this or any other subject. The fact that by 1985 it had sold more than 1,750,000 copies must mean that there is hope for the human race, despite wine merchants' greed in selling their wine too young and despite the shortage of cellarage in most modern accommodation.

Prices are going up the whole time. For that reason I have decided to follow Steven Spurrier's example (in *French Fine Wines* and *French*

Introduction

Country Wines − two other excellent handbooks, both published by Collins Willow Press at £5,95) and code prices alphabetically. Prices given here are approximately those applying at the start of 1986. By the time you read this, no doubt they will be higher, but my comments on each price bracket should have slightly longer application:

Price	*Code*	*Comments*
£1.40–£1.99	A	Mostly rubbish − either heavily pasteurised and almost tasteless reds and sugared, almost tasteless whites, or reds with a strong and usually nasty chemical taste and sour, thin whites. But exceptions can be found: among reds, there are some perfectly respectable Bulgarian Cabernets and Merlots − the product, no doubt, of what is effectively slave labour under the socialist system and dumped at well below production cost. Sainsbury, in 1985, was selling a brilliantly successful Gewürztraminer from Alsace at £1.99. But these wines need searching for, and the quest is not likely to be an enjoyable one.
£2.00–£2.70	B	At this price you begin to find respectable Italian reds (not Chianti, however, in 1986) and some good, medium-weight Spanish red wines from Rioja and Catalonia. The white wine scene is less promising. Muscadets tend to be thin and sharp in price range B, and while it is usually possible to find some fairly good and heavy, nondescriptly fruited Italian whites, you have to shop around among the cheap whites to avoid stomach cramps and bad breath.
£2.70–£3.50	C	This range should be able to cover any but the richest families' requirements for everyday drinking. Excellent Riojas and Chiantis, admirable red Côtes du Rhônes, nothing from Burgundy, but there are some excellently drinkable minor clarets from Haut Médoc and Bordeaux Supérieurs. In this range you begin to find many of the more interesting French country wines, if not yet the more famous ones from the Loire like Bourgueil, Chinon, Sancerre, etc. But there are seriously good red wines being made in Provence, and even if Beaujolais is a bit dicy in this price range you can find Gamays from minor regions like Touraine

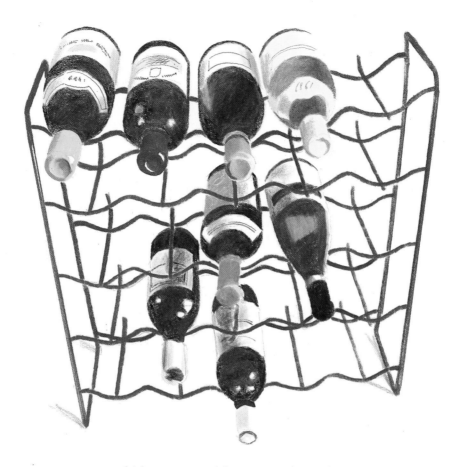

which are quite delicious. Among whites it is no longer possible to find a reasonable Chardonnay in range C but from Alsace you can buy good Rieslings, Gewürztraminers, Muscats, Tokays, and the Germans come in here with their magnificent Kabinetts and Spätleses of 1983. Almost the whole range of Italian wines can be found within this bracket, and the Australians are now making a firm bid with their excellent grape blends – Cabernet-Shiraz, Cabernet-Malbec. A few of the better Australian whites – Chardonnay and Chardonnay-Semillon – may still be found in C bracket, although I suspect not for long. But there are so many excellent wines, and so much abundance of choice, that there is really no reason for the serious wine-drinker ever to leave this range except on special occasions.

£3.50–£4.99   D   This is effectively the last bracket where you will find red wines for instant drinking until you reach G. After D you begin to hit the bracket which should be laid down for at least a couple of years. In this range you have all the better Beaujolais, a few light Burgundies, all the more prestigious French country wines, and most of the best Italian reds; eight-year-old Riojas, some of which, like CVNE's Vina Real, can compare with really hefty wines from the southern Rhône and Burgundy. There are some truly excellent heavy Australian Cabernets and Cabernet-Malbecs which, being shorter on tannin than their Bordeaux equivalents, are usually ready to drink after three or four years; and my own favourite hot country wine, Serge Hochar's famous Château Musar from the Lebanon, a blend of Cabernet Sauvignon, Syrah and, surprisingly, Cinsault. This wine is never sold until it is at least six years old and provides most of the delights of a really heavy Pauillac like Latour at one tenth of the price. Among whites, this price bracket includes all the excellent Chardonnays of southern Burgundy – the Mâcon Villages, whose 1983 vintage made it in many cases the rival of prodigiously expensive wines to the north, and even a few Californian Chardonnays, like Paul Masson's delicious example. Californian reds do not really put in a good showing yet, except their Zinfandels for those who can take the holly berry tang in these beautifully concentrated, spicy wines. Almost no table wine from Portugal costs more than £4.99 at the moment of writing, and there are some splendid Dâo *garrafeiras* of 1970 and even earlier if you can find them. I maintain there is really no need to go beyond D for a dry white table wine, since all the best are represented in this bracket or, occasionally, even lower: Sauvignon from Graves, Bergerac and the Loire; Chardonnays from the Mâconnais, Australia, Northern Italy (sometimes); dry Chenins blancs from South Africa; Rieslings from Alsace and Germany; the very best Muscadets – by no means a contemptible wine in its upper reaches; dry Semillons from Australia. Perhaps the only white grape not represented in this price range is the noble Viognier from the upper Rhône, which makes Condrieu and Château-Grillet – beautiful, rare and expensive wines which must really be left to the rich cognoscenti.

£5.00–£8.00   E   A lot of very dicy wine is sold in this range. The best is all for laying down – Châteauneufs, from the Southern Rhône, minor Hermitages, with Crozes Hermitages and St Josephs for drinking rather sooner; unclassified but known châteaux of Bordeaux, a very few village Burgundies, possibly from the Chalonnais. Californian Cabernet Sauvignons begin to come into their own at this price level, but it is a range to beware: few wines for laying down in price E are really worth laying down, while those for instant drinking are mostly over-priced. Among white wines you have a few *premier cru* Chablis – surely the most over-priced of all popular wines, as a result of the American demand – and a lot of over-rated white Bordeaux.

£8.00–£10.00   F   In the F bracket you may still find most of middle-range Burgundies and Bordeaux for laying down, a few over-priced whites for instant drinking, and a number of oddments from Australia, Italy, Spain and California which have succeeded in making names for themselves in their own countries – by no means always a recommendation. Once again, unless you are laying down wine and have studied the form, or have a wine merchant you trust to advise you, it is a bracket to beware. Many disappointments lurk in it.

£10.00 +   G   All classic, mature wines now cost more than £10 and most of the classic wines for laying down do, too. The first thing is to distinguish one from the other. After that, apply yourself to Hugh Johnson, Oz Clarke's *Webster's Wine Price Guide* and your own experience. Good luck to you.

JANUARY

Most of us tend to wake up on Boxing Day morning with an enormous sigh of relief. At last it is all over and we have a glorious year of respite ahead. We even feel, somewhat optimistically, that the new year is so long that it will never pass and there will never be another Christmas. All we have to do today is to carve the cold turkey or the cold ham, wait for spring, and heat up a few mince pies which will most likely remain uneaten because no one is hungry for such things after all the eating and drinking the day before.

Some of us may have rashly invited the neighbours in to share our leftovers and so when the moment eventually comes to pull the great half-eaten bird from the larder we may look at its cold, rather powdery flesh and think that it deserves a little something to brighten it up and make it more appetising.

There is a tedious joke in the Waugh family, which is traditionally repeated by one or other member of the family each year, about a certain Sir Telford Waugh, first cousin of my father-in-law, Evelyn. When Sir Telford retired from his last posting as Consul-General in Ankara he wrote a book of memoirs entitled *Turkey Yesterday, Today and Tomorrow* which Arthur Waugh, Evelyn's father, wittily remarked should have been called Boxing Day. Although neither Evelyn Waugh nor his son, Bron, has ever been particularly short of jokes of his own, both of them seem to have taken a perverse delight in repeating yearly Arthur Waugh's *bon mot*.

Perhaps it is the deadening, loathsome truth of the remark that has made it so attractive to succeeding generations of Waughs. Or perhaps they, in their arrogance, are amazed to have sprung from the loins of one whose wit was so laboured. Be that as it may, I very much doubt that, so long as I share my life with any member of the Waugh family, I will spend a Boxing Day without hearing about Sir Telford. It is a small price to pay.

So, as I muse about Sir Telford Waugh and my half-eaten turkey, I think that perhaps Boxing Day needs a little livening up.

One of the nicest ways of heating up turkey, in my opinion, is to mince it and mix it into a thick, creamy béchamel sauce flavoured with nutmeg and to serve it with croûtons of fried bread and brussels sprouts.

Minced ham on the other hand can be made into a mousse or a soufflé. A ham soufflé takes considerably longer to cook than a cheese or sweet one but it is good and filling. It can be a little dry and so could well be served with Cumberland sauce.

We all love baked potatoes. At least I have yet to come across anyone who does not. So stick to them. In any case Boxing Day is hardly the day on which to embark on varieties of *Pommes de terre à la boulangère*. Very filling and rich things will not necessarily be wanted. But make a delicious fresh salad. It will be so welcome after all the stuffing and brandy butter that went on yesterday.

One of my favourite winter salads is made from a mixture of beetroot, celery and *mâche* or lamb's lettuce. Lamb's lettuce is easily found in London and other big towns. Or if you live in the country you can scatter a packet of seeds in your garden and you will find that the lamb's lettuce grows easily. Allow some of it to go to seed and you will never be short of it in future. It is closely related to forget-me-not and it perpetuates itself as easily as forget-me-nots do. However, I would not advise eating forget-me-nots.

Another good winter salad, and a particularly refreshing one too, is made from what I call endive, but what other people call chicory – anyway the long, white, pointed ones – watercress and thinly sliced orange. Although I am ceaselessly warning people against the indiscriminate use of avocado pears, I do think that they make an excellent salad when mixed with watercress. Apart from anything else, the mixture is very pretty.

For those who prefer coleslaw, a finely shredded white cabbage should be dressed with a mixture of lemon juice, fresh cream and mustard. A handful of sultanas can be added to the cabbage. Then there are of course all the endless versions of red cabbage salad. The cabbage should be sliced very finely – it somehow reminds one of hardship, bleak northern climes and the Brothers Grimm. To it can be added nuts, onions, garlic, sliced apple or celery, or the whole lot. Sometimes I find the thought of red cabbage salad infinitely depressing, but I do think that it goes particularly well with either cold turkey or cold pork.

Supposing when you have eaten your cold turkey or ham soufflé and delicious salad you want to show off with a slightly festive pudding, you could make some *croûtes au madère*. Fry some pieces of bread cut into neat round shapes with a pastry cutter, spread them with apricot jam and keep warm. Just before serving pour over them some mixed dried fruits which have been stewing gently in white wine with a good spoonful of apricot jam and to which you have added half a glass of madeira at the last minute. Serve the *croûtes au madère* with thick cream.

If you prefer something less rich, bake some whole small oranges very, very slowly in the oven with water and sugar. Ginger snaps are particularly good with these oranges. When it comes to the cheese, don't just serve Stilton. There are those, like myself, who regard it as an over-rated cheese. I know that most people love it, but the prospect of Stilton yesterday, today and tomorrow fills me with gloom. Have a large piece of Emmenthal on offer too, then by evening you may have quite enjoyed your Boxing Day fare and you may even be looking forward to tomorrow's *fricassé*.

With a good five days to go between Boxing Day and New Year's Eve, you should have time to rest your stomach and regain your appetite in time to appreciate the festivities which may attend the dying year.

It is strange how to a child each New Year's Day seems to be invested with some special significance whereas to an adult New Year's Day seems much like any other winter's day unless of course, as a good Catholic, he celebrates the Feast of the Circumcision and attends Mass. Apart from that, New Year's Day merely seems to prompt a few gloomy folk to remark that they certainly hope that this year will be better than last year. It could hardly be much worse. And as for New Year's Eve, well that just presents another opportunity for a booze up and for a jolly good dinner – perhaps even a party to celebrate the end of the festive season.

It is far easier to eat cold than hot food when standing up, so I would avoid a hot stew even in darkest winter unless my guests were to be comfortably seated around a large table, and as for lasagne it really has become a little too popular. Perhaps, if you feel that cold food is too chilling an approach to a happy winter's evening, you might start by serving a hot thick soup.

Minestrone, if properly cooked with enough vegetables – not forgetting celery and spinach – is delicious, but very filling. A thick, creamy potato or parsnip soup might be better, and I have never met anyone who disliked artichoke soup.

Since garlic bread is no trouble to make, it could well be served as an accompaniment to your soup. The mediocre dough which passes in England for a "French stick" can only be improved by being sliced halfway through at intervals, stuffed with butter and garlic and heated.

To my mind one of the main disadvantages of buffet food is that people seem to think it necessary to produce umpteen different dishes. The greedy guest whose eyes are too big for his stomach will then pile something of everything onto his plate. Haricot beans will collide with chicken in mayonnaise. Cold rice and tuna fish, floppy quiches and cold sausages will fight for supremacy. "How delicious, Jane!" the polite guests will cry as they force the ill-assorted food down unwilling throats.

So, above all, keep it simple. What could be better than the finest cold beef, home-cooked gammon in cider with brown sugar and cloves, and a fine selection of salads? But, if you insist on having a hot main course, you could do worse than serve a great dish of risotto made with chicken livers, bacon, onions, carrots, courgettes, garlic and peas; or a Suleimann's Pilau, a risotto made with chicken or mutton, onions and sultanas and served with yoghurt.

I recently went to a dinner party for some sixty-five people in France. We were given a most delicious variation of chicken in mayonnaise. Remove the roast chicken from the bone and chop the meat into smallish pieces. Make a mayonnaise with a lot of lemon juice. Mix the chicken, some sultanas and fine pieces of lemon peel into the mayonnaise. Decorate the top with a generous amount of roast, split almonds. Serve with a slightly bitter salad – preferably chicory or endive.

One of the best party dishes I know is a cake made of layers of pancakes with ham, mayonnaise and lettuce or chicken and mayonnaise. The cake must be sliced with a sharp knife before it is served or it will slide about everywhere.

If you are ambitious and are feeling particularly festive, you could always attempt the traditional old dish of stuffing a goose with a pheasant with a wild duck with a partridge with a quail, but unless you are both gifted and patient you will probably have to ask your butcher to bone the birds for you. Then pot roast them very slowly with a little wine and the usual mixture of vegetables and herbs. I have a brother who regularly delights us all with this exquisite dish. It can be served hot but I think it is infinitely better cold and far easier to carve. As this is a rich dish, I would serve it with nothing more than green salad and perhaps a salad made from sliced oranges, a little sliced onion, pepper and olive oil.

Then what about a pudding? Some will always stick to chocolate mousse. But do not make it with gelatine and always use chocolate Menier. I would prefer a beautiful fruit tart. For an apple tart, spread the pastry with finely sieved apple purée into which you have stirred a little marmalade. Cover the apple purée with some finely sliced and peeled eating apples and glaze with apricot jam. Nothing is more elegant than a well-made apple tart. Eschew the fancy china pastry cases. The tin ones with loose bottoms are far more satisfactory. And do remember one good pudding is enough. Your guests do not want to have to make decisions, nor do you want to be left with a fridge full of soggy meringues and stale cream.

Once we have celebrated New Year there is nothing left but to settle down and patiently wait for January and February to go away. The prospect seems bleak and, worst of all, the long, grey English winter threatens us with months of dull vegetables. So many people are haunted by memories of the vinegary beetroot, boiled cabbage stalks and lumps of swede which they were forced to eat every day at school, that they can never again look a cabbage or a beetroot, let alone a swede, in the face. But these vegetables do not really have to be so dull, indeed I am of the opinion that fresh winter vegetables well cooked are always preferable to frozen peas, beans or even spinach.

Turnips, for instance, are another scourge of school lunches, but they can be chopped into small cubes and melted slowly in butter with salt, pepper and a little brown sugar until they are thoroughly cooked. About half a cup of water should be added just to prevent them from burning and a chopped cooking apple enhances their flavour. Turnips are delicious served with duck or pork. I think people sometimes think they are about to eat potatoes and so they get a nasty shock with the first mouthful.

Swedes can be cooked in the same way until they are thoroughly mushy. They need a great deal of pepper and would not necessarily benefit from the addition of an apple.

Beetroots are certainly among my favourite vegetables. I do not know why beetroots are often sold ready cooked since they only have to be boiled in their skins for quite a long time, depending on their size. The skins come off with no difficulty once they are cooked. Beetroot in white sauce is not only delicious but beautiful and makes an excellent first course. The white sauce should be well flavoured with grated nutmeg. Equally, the juice of half a lemon and some good thick cream can be poured over hot, sliced beetroot. A handful of chopped parsley should be sprinkled over it, and once again a little grated nutmeg.

Carrots are delicious if cooked in a little water with some butter and a teaspoonful of sugar. Ideally they ought to be cooked by the time the water has evaporated so that they can caramelize slightly in the remaining butter and sugar then add a good handful of chopped parsley.

Instead of the usual roast potatoes, try surrounding your joint with a mixture of diced potatoes, carrots and thinly sliced onions. A little oil should be poured over the vegetables and a sprig of rosemary buried in them. The result is quite excellent.

Fresh, green, boiled cabbage with a little butter, pepper and salt can be wonderful. It can even be something one longs for but there is no doubt that by January, if not before, it begins to pall. For variety, fry a chopped onion and some chopped bacon in butter. Add the cooked cabbage, turn it over in the butter, season, add a couple of tablespoonfuls of cream and two or three pounded juniper berries. Red cabbage makes an occasional welcome change and is a good accompaniment for a stew, with a baked potato.

Slice the red cabbage as finely as possible, add a tablespoonful of brown sugar, some butter, a little vinegar, the juice of an orange, a chopped cooking apple, a little water to prevent burning, two or three cloves, salt, pepper and garlic and cook slowly for about three quarters of an hour at least.

Leeks are usually more popular than other winter vegetables. As everyone knows, they are delicious in cheese sauce. I think that like this they should be served as a first course rather than as an accompaniment, since gravy and cheese sauce are rather unwelcome when running into each other.

Very few people make good mashed potatoes, or *purée de pommes de terre* – purée being the key word. The potatoes must be floury ones and should be boiled with salt, an onion and a large clove of garlic. They will never be fine enough unless a sieve is used. Add a large lump of butter, a good deal of pepper and more salt, beat until the butter has melted and then adding the milk, beating all the time. The purée should be smooth, quite runny and fluffy. It will dry out a little if it is kept warm, but some more milk may be added at the last minute. Otherwise, if the purée is really well beaten and fluffy it can be put in a soufflé dish and left in a fairly hot oven, then it will rise a little and go brown on top.

In fact there is a great deal that can be said about potatoes and there are a great many ways of cooking them – all delicious – so we should every day on our knees thank God for Sir John Hawkins who introduced them into England in 1563.

I found in France a delicious recipe for a *gâteau de pommes de terre* which might be the very thing for a dull winter's evening. Mix some well-mashed potatoes with a little béchamel sauce, some grated Gruyère, the yolks of four eggs and then add the beaten whites of the eggs. Cook the mixture in a soufflé dish in a bain-marie for about an hour and serve accompanied by a tomato sauce. Another type of potato cake can be made by slicing the potatoes into rounds and putting them in layers into a buttered soufflé dish. Between the potato layers put little pieces of butter, salt and pepper. Cover the dish with buttered paper and cook in the oven for about three quarters of an hour. Turn the potatoes out of the soufflé dish before serving.

The more one thinks about potatoes, the more one is obliged to marvel at their infinite variety. Think of potato soup and conjure up the desert we lived in before good Sir John introduced them. It is almost impossible for us to imagine meals without potatoes, especially during these dull winter months, and although William Shakespeare may have eaten them – they took several decades to become established – Chaucer can never have had the pleasure and his

Franklin in those house it "snewed of mete and drinke" and "of all deyntees that men coude thinke" missed out on potatoes.

Potatoes were not popularized in France until the end of the eighteenth century when the economist and agronomist Antoine-Augustin Parmentier wrote about them in a thesis on vegetables to be used in times of food shortage, and now the *Larousse Gastronomique* devotes no fewer than nineteen columns to them. So there is really no need to fall back on the frozen pea except in desperation.

I cannot remember when I was last given a suet pudding, although I do remember a rather bitter altercation on the subject. My youngest sister-in-law was due to be married in the middle of June. Her husband is American and his family were to cross the Herring Pond for the celebrations. There was some discussion in our family as to what typically English dish would most please the visiting Americans. Now, by coincidence, my eldest sister-in-law is also married to an American and has lived in the United States for some twenty odd years. She it was who suggested a steak and kidney pudding. Furious objections were immediately raised. No one in their right mind would want to eat steak and kidney pudding in the middle of the summer.

"Summer!" ejaculated my oldest sister-in-law indignantly. "No American arriving in England in June would have any idea that this was what you call summer."

The battle raged fiercely for several days but eventually the "antis" prevailed and the marriage was celebrated during a week-end of glorious June sunshine and without any steak and kidney pudding.

I was certainly among the antis. The weather may often be cold in England in June, but I am not prepared to admit to Americans or to anyone else for that matter that we always expect it to be so.

However, January is a different matter altogether and there is nothing which I would welcome more readily in January than a steak and kidney pudding – or a roly-poly pudding.

For your roly-poly pudding, roll your suet pastry out to an oblong shape. Lay smoked back bacon rashes along it, sprinkle with melted chopped onion and some mixed chopped herbs. Roll up your pudding, wrap it in buttered silver foil and cook in a steamer for three hours. Serve with a thick tomato sauce.

Savoury dumplings are another winter pleasure. Make the dumplings in the usual way but incorporate into them some chopped, fried bacon and onion and some thyme. Cook and serve the dumplings either in a stew or in a good chicken or game broth.

For those with a sweet tooth, perhaps the most wonderful treat in the world is a good, old-fashioned apple-hat: a suet pudding filled with sliced apples and golden syrup.

It is easy to overlook the joys of puddings. Those wily *parlez-vous* have taught us of the idle joys of cheese and fruit, but I maintain that a great many people who say that they don't like puddings really mean that they can't be bothered to make them.

I have discovered something else – which is that people who drink a lot have so much sugar in their blood stream that they genuinely do not feel the need for more. So when you hear your best friend saying that he never touches puddings, there may be more to it than meets the eye. In any case children who are below the age of alcoholic consent always love puddings – and so, I hasten to add, do I. Especially apple hat in January.

January Wines

The great problem with Christmas guests is how to get rid of them. As fewer and fewer places of work open in the week between Christmas and New Year, guests show less and less inclination to leave. There is no earthly reason why one should go on pouring one's best wine down their throats day after day; if one did, it would have the effect of inducing them to stay longer, as well as seriously depleting one's cellar. This is the time of year I visit my "sin bin" – the part of the cellar which contains all the wines I regret having bought, or which have gone off. Nearly every wine-drinker has his equivalent of a sin bin, at whatever level he buys his wine. My own contains some 1969 clarets with quite respectable names and even some 1973s, a number of 1975 Châteauneuf du Papes, a huge assortment of minor Bordeaux which I thought might be a bargain, did not like and have now kept too long, as well as a surprising variety of Chablis, white Burgundy and minor Sauternes which I foolishly bought from a wine merchant's list on their labels alone, untasted. In other cases I may have bought some wine experimentally for a dinner party, not liked it and been left with a bottle or two. This is the moment to bring them out, in ascending order of nastiness. I once found a bottle of such indescribable filth that I complained about it in the most exaggerated terms, and the wine merchant concerned sent me another bottle derisively. It is made by Angelo Papagni at Madera in the San Joaquin area of California from a grape called Alicante Bouschet, tasting of nail varnish with an undertow of diesel exhaust. I am keeping it as my *coup de grâce* for the Christmas guest who has not left by Epiphany.

But, apart from the need to speed the parting guests, life goes on in the lean days between Christmas and New Year. Sometimes people come to the house for a meal, and one does not particularly wish to insult them. Sometimes one is left gloriously alone with one's life's companion and cook; then the need to produce the best wine with the strange, post-festive diet of cold and reheated Christmas food becomes paramount. Actually, I tend to take myself off to a fat-farm in Tring, Hertfordshire, eating and drinking nothing for a week to purge the excesses of the Christmas season. That is the greatest self-indulgence of all. But I leave my dear wife and children some advice about what they may like to drink in my absence.

Any wine goes perfectly well with cold turkey and indeed cold meat of any sort, but I feel that really good, expensive wines are wasted on it. Even Beaujolais is too rich. I would suggest a light, inexpensive claret from the Côtes de Bourg or Blaye or a Fronsac, a Bergerac or one of the reds from Entre-deux-Mers. Equally a light Rioja, such as Vina Alberdi, available from Laymont and Shaw in Truro or, sometimes, from Sainsbury's. There is no earthly point in going beyond price range C for wines with cold meat.

Re-heated turkey in a fricassée should be accompanied by a Kabinett or even a Spätlese from the Rhine or Mosel. There is no short-cut to either of these wines. I have yet to find a decent Riesling from Australia, and the New Zealand examples strike me as pretty foul. Where the turkey is minced with béchamel and nutmeg, I feel the delicacy of the riesling grape might be impugned, and suggest one of the light red Cabernet Franc wines from the Loire – a Bourgueil or its little-known, cheaper and quite excellent little sister, a Thouarsais (available from Yapp Bros of Mere, Wiltshire). Even a Chinon might fight itself in conflict with the nutmeg.

I adore ham soufflé, but if it is served with Cumberland sauce it becomes impossible to match with any wine. Cider would be the best drink, for those who can get it down. Without the Cumberland sauce, I would suggest the richest and oldest Châteauneuf you can find. The best on the market, currently, is Jaboulet's magnificent Châteauneuf du Pape Les Cèdres 1967, available at a huge price from Loeb in Jermyn Street – they also sold a stupefying Gigondas 1967 until recently – but there are some pretty good Beaucastels 1970 floating around. But Châteauneuf – and Gigondas – is a classic example of a wine which is quite cheap to lay down – since 1976 all vintages except 1977 and 1984 have been pretty good, and 1978 was brilliant. You lay it down at D or low E and you drink it at G ten or fifteen years later. Buying old Châteauneuf is both expensive and risky, since you do not always know how it has been stored. Soon, I imagine, it will be as unprocurable as old Burgundy.

It is a waste of time to drink expensive Sauternes or Barsac with any dessert as sweet as *Croûte au madère*. They come out as dry wines, which destroys the whole point of them. Possibly the only wine to drink with puddings of this sort (apart from champagne, which goes with everything) is one of the intensely sweet near-Sauternes which are just beginning to put in a appearance on the English market – a Monbazillac or a Loupiac. They are also much cheaper than Sauternes, which is an advantage. All these dessert wines go well with strong cheese, too – the only wine which does so, apart from port. For some reason it has become almost universally accepted in England that you can drink a hefty Burgundy with Camembert, Brie or Stilton. You can't. The cheeses absolutely kill the wine, producing a taste of tin and ammonia. Even Gruyère or Emmenthal can spoil the taste of a dry wine, although the hard English cheeses go well with almost anything.

I will deal with the almost impossible question of what wine, if any, to drink with soup in the next chapter. For the rest of the January recommendations, I must admit that I am not particularly fond of rice and tuna fish salad, but find it is improved by a crisp, dry Sauvignon to cut through the greasiness of it: either a white Bordeaux from the Graves without too much Semillon in it – the new methods of cold fermentation are producing some very good and reasonably priced wine nowadays with plenty of fruit and none of that dreadful, tired, cardboardy taste which the trade calls "oak". Otherwise go to the Loire for a rich, gooseberry-leaf-flavoured Sancerre in the D range, its slightly cheaper neighbour, in Ménétou-Salon; or a Pouilly Fumé which will probably be in E. The 1983s are magnificent, but do not need keeping, and the 1984s are equally ready.

With risottos I would recommend any heavy red wine from the Rhône or Provence. In fact hot rice is a brilliant accompaniment to even the most expensive reds, so long as there are not too many raisins or curried effects in it. Even juniper, coriander and cumin do not spoil my own beloved Château Musar from the Lebanon, but an old Châteauneuf, Gigondas or Cornas would be just as good. Bandol is another well-established, hefty wine which can take most spices on board, but more and more of these delicious, heavy wines, often from a Cabernet-Sauvignon-Syrah mixture, are being developed by the experimental growers of Provence. Robin Yapp, of Mere, has some splendid examples.

Mayonnaise presents problems, as do all preponderantly egg dishes, since no wine goes very well with eggs. My own experience suggests that a slightly sharp Chardonnay is best with mayonnaise – not one of the magnificent, buttery Californian Chardonnays nor even a massive wine from Beaune, but perhaps a little village Chablis from an "off" year or a very young Mâconnais. The Italians are producing some fairly good Chardonnays nowadays in the north, between Venice and

Trieste, or one of their Pinot Biancos or Pinot Grigios might do – all in the B price range.

I should go to Italy, also for an inexpensive accompaniment to steak and kidney pudding, roly-poly pudding or any savoury suet. It is my own experience that the merlot grape goes best with suet – in France, they hardly know about it – which might mean a St Emilion or a Pomerol, but everything from Pomerol is over-priced since the Americans discovered about it and a St Emilion might be slightly lost in the suet. But the northern Italians, again, are turning out excellently concentrated, rather coarse Merlots which soften within eighteen months or two years. One of the best is called Merlot di Pramaggiore, in the B-C range, obtainable from Recount Wines of Lower Sloane Street. If the roly-poly pudding is accompanied by a tomato-based sauce, I would forget about Merlot and go straight for a cheap Chianti Putto in the B range. These Chiantis vary a little from year to year – there was practically none made in 1984 – but they keep a consistently drinkable standard for the most part. For some reason which I have never identified – perhaps it is just force of habit – I always tend towards Chianti when there is tomato sauce around. I can't explain it, and know little enough about the Italian grapes in any case. I can only say it works.

With sweet suet puddings like apple hat I should try a rich old auslese but one with enough acid in it to cut through the suet. At the moment of writing, Peter Hallgarten still has a huge stock of 1976 ausleses, and would no doubt be happy to advise. If there are a lot of cloves in the apple hat, try a *vendage tardive* Gewürztraminer from Alsace. Loeb has a few. With treacle pudding, I am afraid there is no wine yet invented which will either improve or complement it. Try water. The same is true of chocolate mousse, although I met a madman once who said he always drank Calvados with chocolate mousse. I have not tried it and so do not know if he is right. I record the fact that he was mad merely as background information. Of course champagne goes with everything, and chocolate mousse might provide an opportunity to try one of the *demi-secs* which the French have always rather liked and which are beginning to find their way into the English market, being rather popular with university students. The effect of even bitter chocolate is to turn the *demi-sec* into an *extra-sec* or *brut*, which is really what one wants. Personally, I seldom eat chocolate mousse.

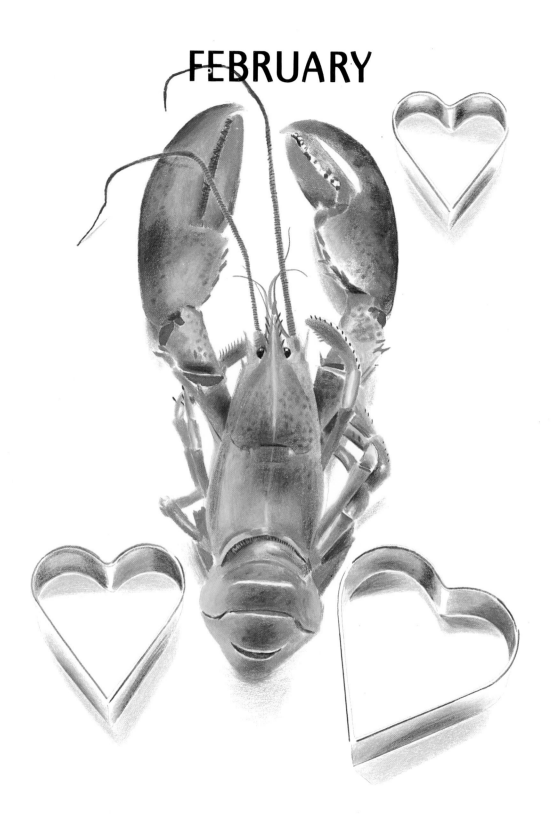
FEBRUARY

There is little to celebrate during the two gloomy months which follow Christmas. Close students of the Church calendar may wish to remember St Praejectus or Prix, bishop and martyr on January 25, or Blessed Elizabeth of Mantua, virgin, on February 20, but most of us lesser mortals are left with St Valentine, and, depending on the date of Easter, Mardi Gras or Shrove Tuesday.

So I suppose St Valentine's Day could provide an occasion for a really exquisite dinner for two. Make sure that your guest is not one of those people who only really appreciate things which are either expensive or out of season, or both. There is nothing more dispiriting than cooking for such Philistines.

If, like myself, you often have to cook for large numbers of hungry people, you may be attracted to the idea of cooking a delicate meal for two, once in a while.

Take a look, then, at *Les recettes originales de Michel Guérard* in *La Grande Cuisine Minceur* and your mouth will water. Do not think I am in favour of slimming. I am not. There is nothing more revolting than a skinny woman eating steak in London or Paris while the Third World starves. But, whether you are fat or thin, *La Grande Cuisine Minceur* makes appetising reading and the pictures will make you drool.

One of the most tempting of Michel Guérard's first courses is *oeuf poule au caviar* in which he describes how to fill egg shells with a mixture of delicately scrambled egg, a little chopped onion, chives and cream cheese. A spoonful of caviar is put on top of this. The top of the eggshell is then replaced, leaving the caviar visible.

What could be more delicious to follow with than *homard au cresson*? The lobster is served on a bed of puréed watercress and sorrel, with a delicate wine and mushroom sauce. I think I might be tempted to leave out the mushrooms myself. I don't think that their rightful place is beside watercress. Once you have this book in your hand you will find endless enticing recipes, but remember you will also have your work cut out because Monsieur Guérard's recipes have a tendency to refer you to page 300 and back again.

In France in recent years I have discovered a new fashion for serving hot goat's cheese and it might be a good thing to do at your "dinner for two", particularly as the cheese needs to be put under the grill at the last moment which makes it a nuisance at a large dinner party. In advance prepare a bed of salad on each plate – chicory or endive or a mixture of both would be nice at this time of year. Pour over a little dressing made of olive oil or sunflower oil and lemon juice. (A strong olive oil might not suit the cheese.) Have ready two slices cut from a goat's cheese, preferably one of the long, round variety. When you are ready for your cheese, put it under the grill for an instant until it is hot, beginning to bubble and turning golden. Put the cheese slices on the salad and serve immediately.

What is the most delicious "pudding" you can dream of? I have mentioned apple hat, but that is hardly suitable for your *dîner à deux*. One of my other favourite puddings is a flourless lemon or orange soufflé (Elizabeth David's recipe in *French Country Cooking*), but alas you would have to abandon your guest while you noisily whipped the egg whites. So leave that for another day.

It being St Valentine's Day, perhaps the most suitable *entremets* would be *petits coeurs à la crème*. These can be made in a variety of ways. Allow your milk to go sour. When the curds seem to be completely separated from the whey (it will take several days), strain them through heart-shaped moulds lined with muslin. Serve with cream and tinned figs or guavas.

Of course, if the heart theme really excites you, you could serve a salad of artichoke hearts as a first course, then, Boccaccio-like, you could have sauté-ed heart, follow that with the heart-shaped, Camembert-style cheese known as *coeur de Neufchâtel*, then have your *petits coeurs à la crème* for dessert.

For the heart, make sure that all the sinewy bits are removed. Dice it into small pieces and sauté it in sizzling, good quality butter. Flamber with brandy, add a teaspoonful of Dijon mustard, some sliced mushrooms if you like, salt, pepper, three or four tablespoonfuls of double cream, and simmer gently for five or six minutes. Sprinkle with a generous handful of chopped parsley and serve with rice. Wash the whole lot down with Chambolle-Musigny Les Amoureuses.

*

Considering how much most people like pancakes, it is surprising how rarely one eats them. Perhaps this is because they are thought to be rather a nuisance to make – but make them you should whenever Shrove Tuesday comes around.

Two or three years ago my daughter brought me a wonderful present back from France. It looks like an extremely fat ping-pong bat but is, in fact, an electric crêpe-maker. It has many advantages. For one thing the kitchen no longer stinks of fat when I make pancakes, the pancakes do not have to be tossed so there is no more cursing and sweating, and above all my crêpe-maker produces the thinnest and most even pancakes imaginable. Strangely enough I know of no one else in England who has such a toy although they are available in the big London shops and are infinitely enjoyable to use. If you have one you will never again overlook Shrove Tuesday.

One of the most unusual and best recipes I know for pancakes comes from Argentina and was given me by a French friend. It sounds rather disgusting and I would never have tried it had I not complete confidence in my friend's good taste.

Make a pile of about eight pancakes and put a layer of well-cooked, chopped spinach flavoured with nutmeg and garlic between each. Pour béchamel sauce over the whole thing, cover the top with dark brown sugar and put it under the grill. This can be kept warm for a little while in a low oven. In order to make it into more of a main course, I tried putting a slice of ham on top of each layer of spinach. It was very good.

Another French friend once gave me, as a first course, cold pancakes folded in two with a slice of smoked salmon in the middle and served with a quarter of lemon. This seemed faintly shocking at first, but it was good.

There is no end to the things a Breton will do with a pancake. My same daughter once came back from an exchange visit to Brittany having eaten pancakes stuffed in different ways every day for a fortnight. The best, she thought, was a pancake sandwich with a fried egg and a piece of ham in the middle.

A wonderful pancake dish which I have already mentioned as suitable for a buffet and which never fails to please although it is possibly more suitable for summer is made in layers as follows: pancake, lettuce, mayonnaise, pancake, ham, pancake, sliced tomato, mayonnaise and so forth. No more than eight pancakes should be used to make one "cake" which as I have said should be cut, like a cake, with a sharp knife by the cook before his or her friends are given the opportunity of making a dreadful mess. The dish really is much better if proper green, Greek or Tuscan olive oil is used for the mayonnaise.

Anyone who uses their imagination can think up a filling for a pancake, using spinach, mushrooms, chicken or ham. For instance, to some minced ham add sliced mushrooms cooked in butter, a little béchamel, some thick cream, grated nutmeg and a teaspoonful of Dijon mustard. It is important not to make the filling too dry, particularly as, in my opinion, it is a mistake to cover the pancakes with more sauce. For one thing, if you do, no one can see what they are eating. The alternative is to sprinkle them with grated cheese, add a few dots of butter and warm them up in the oven. Pancakes suffer neither from being frozen nor from being warmed up, but I would freeze them without their fillings.

One of the simplest ways of turning a pancake into an elegant pudding is to fill it with expensive strawberry jam to which you have added a squeeze of lemon juice. Put the rolled-up pancakes into a flat dish, keep them warm and sprinkle them with grilled split almonds before serving. English people tend to think that cream has to be poured over every pudding. I think this is a grave mistake, but in this case it is advisable, particularly if, as I do, you live in the West Country and are surrounded by herds of beautiful doe-eyed Jersey cows.

My younger son is firmly of the belief that the best pancakes are traditional, plain ones, served with sugar and a squeeze of lemon. He may well be right and in any case I tend to agree that the simplest things are often the best.

At this time of year a person's fancy may easily turn to soups, even if that person, like myself, is not particularly keen on them. I rather agree with a friend who described soup as a waste of good eating space.

Nevertheless I have in my house some fine soup tureens and a husband with a passion for any soup you care to mention.

Once I left him alone with our children for two weeks in February while I went to India. When I returned full of talk about the Mogul Empire, the great God Shiva and the Taj Mahal by moonlight I found the whole family obsessed by fish soup. They could talk and think of nothing else and to this day – several years have passed – a dreamy look comes into the children's eyes when they remember the fish soup their father cooked. There was clearly no question at the time of "children dear were we long alone? The sea grows stormy the little ones moan." Certainly not. That fish soup possessed them, body and soul. They seem to have spent days preparing it. If you ask any of them now how it was made they look knowing and mysterious as the great God Shiva himself and say that they cannot remember. Occasionally they mutter "saffron" or "lobster shells". Was it thickened, you ask them? Oh yes, they nod wisely. How did they thicken it? They have no idea. In any case they clearly enjoyed it almost as much as I enjoyed my Indian holiday.

Another memorable fish soup was made one day after we had been for a walk by the seaside on the coast of Somerset. There we met a young fisherman who had caught no fewer than three huge skate. We were gazing in admiration at his catch when he offered to give us one of the enormous fish. No, no, we couldn't possibly accept so generous a present. But he insisted. He loved fishing but hated fish so he usually gave what he caught to his granny. His granny could clearly not eat three whole skate by next week-end when he would be fishing again.

The bones of that fish formed the basis of a very fine bouillabaisse.

I suppose that most people quite rightly associate bouillabaisse with the Mediterranean and the summer, but since fish soup is generally rather filling and therefore warming, there seems to be no very good reason why it should not be eaten all the year round – and particularly in winter.

What must be the worst poem in the English language is a poem by Thackeray inspired by bouillabaisse, and one wonders if this reflects the leaden, uninspired quality of the soup or the inadequacies of Thackeray as a poet. I cannot help thinking that the blame lies with the poet:

This Bouillabaisse a noble dish is –
A sort of soup or broth or brew
Or hotch potch of all sorts of fishes . . .

Of course a *real* bouillabaisse must be made with the right mixture of Mediterranean fish like rascasse and St Pierre but it is wrong to suppose that Atlantic white fish may not be substituted for these. Even in the south of France the ingredients vary widely. Some insist on mussels and squid and others will tell you that these have no place in the genuine article as eaten in the *Vieux Port* in Marseilles. As far as I am concerned, the important thing is to make a delicious soup along the lines of bouillabaisse, call it what you will and enjoy it.

Basically what you need to do is to make a soup by melting some chopped onions, leeks, herbs, garlic and a couple of pieces of tomato in oil. Add boiling water or preferably fish stock made from the bones of a fresh skate presented to you by a stranger on the sea-shore. Add the potatoes and the various fish and cook until tender. The fish and potatoes are generally served separately from the soup which is served in its turn with slices of toast and aioli.

Of course you may prefer a more conventional soup at this time of year. Something more immediately associated with the north, the cold and the grey skies. In that case your mind is likely to turn to something more like potato soup or lentil soup.

The most popular soup I have ever come across in my life is cockie-leekie soup. Different people may make it in different ways. I merely melt the chopped leeks in butter, add the diced potatoes, salt and pepper and cook the whole lot quite slowly in chicken stock. I know that some people think that only water should be used as stock takes away from the purity of the vegetables, and some might believe in putting the soup through a sieve as one would for *potage bonne-femme* made in the same way but with carrots as well as a few leeks. And there is no doubt about it that thick soups are always better served with croutons. The good thing about croutons is that they can be made in advance and kept warm – or even re-heated in the oven.

One of the most traditional and best of French soups is a vegetable soup or *garbure*. Mapie de Toulouse-Lautrec in her excellent cookery book *La Cuisine de Mapie* gives a recipe for a *garbure Béarnaise*.

Mapie de Toulouse-Lautrec came from the same family as the painter and was a descendant of the Counts of Toulouse – great feudal lords of the Languedoc – and her recipes belong to the very best

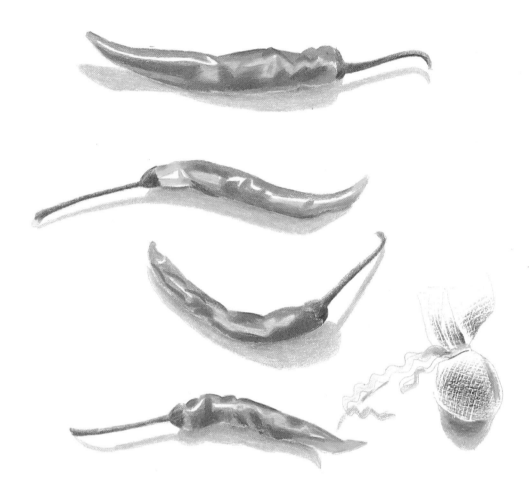

tradition of French household cooking. A French friend of ours, and a distant cousin of Mapie's, remembers being taken as a child by his father to lunch with her in her house in Biarritz. Mapie was enormously fat which was hardly surprising as she apparently spent her entire life eating.

Anyway, here is her recipe for *garbure*.

Peel and chop your potatoes roughly and put them with the previously soaked haricot beans into boiling salted water in an earthenware dish – according to Mapie a metal saucepan takes away from the delicacy of the taste. Add a *bouquet garni*, with half a red chilli which takes the place of pepper. Add garlic and marjoram. Simmer for two hours and then add two chopped cabbages, cover the pot and continue cooking. One hour before serving add a piece of *confit d'oie* or a piece of bacon. Place some thick, sliced stale bread in the bottom of your soup tureen and pour the soup, from which you have removed the *bouquet garni* and the chilli, over the bread. The soup should be so thick that the ladle will stand up alone in the middle of the tureen.

It is easy to imagine Mapie's huge bulk moving stealthily about her old French kitchen as she watched greedily over the various stages of her *garbure*, eating and eating all the time. It is not so easy to imagine today's woman executive rushing home from her office, dressed in her best suit from Next, having had all of two crispbreads and a cup of coffee for lunch, ready to turn her hand to a *garbure Béarnaise*. Nevertheless I think she should have a go. I'm sure it would make her feel more relaxed. There has indeed passed away a glory from this earth.

One last word about Mapie's *garbure*. Almost everyone in France cooks on gas so they can easily use an earthernware dish but of course this is not the case in England where so many people use electricity. But I wonder how many palates are really so refined as to be able to tell the difference between *garbure* cooked in earthenware and *garbure* cooked in metal. As for the *confit d'oie* or preserved goose, you can find it tinned in various shops in London but I myself would be perfectly happy to use bacon.

Lentil and split pea soup really seem like pale shadows of the proper thing compared to a good *garbure*. But the French have another excellent way of serving soup. Cook a *pot au feu* or boil a fresh tongue with the usual vegetables and serve the stock first as soup and then the meat for your main course.

In England there is a new – to me – extraordinarily delicious soup going around which is made from carrots and oranges. I have had this soup made from two different recipes – one of them is in the Magimix handbook – and both are equally delicious. For the other recipe, melt a chopped onion and a pound of chopped carrots in butter. Add stock, salt and pepper and simmer until the vegetables are cooked. Sieve the vegetables and add the grated rind of one orange and the juice of two, a little brown sugar and a drop of tabasco. Serve with cream and chopped parsley.

Apart from this, there are many old favourites which should not be forgotten, like Jerusalem artichoke soup which I for one love but rarely make. The reason why I rarely make it is simply because I am lazy. My vegetable garden is quite a long way away from my house and apart from picking brussels sprouts in a hard frost there is nothing more depressing than digging up artichokes in the cold when the ground is either muddy or frozen solid. As a result of my laziness and because artichokes spread rapidly, I suppose that before long my whole garden will be overtaken by them. Those of you who are not lucky enough to have vegetable gardens will not of course be beset by this particular problem.

One soup of which I must admit to being exceedingly fond is bortsch or beetroot soup and once again there are various ways of making it and each person will swear that theirs is the best, the original and probably the only way. I used to make it rather thinly with a great deal of sour cream put in at the last minute, but I have since had a much better version made to the recipe of a real Pole so I can only assume that besides being a better version it is also a more genuine one.

In fact if one thinks about it hard enough, there is practically nothing which cannot be made into soup. I once spent a very long time making some rather nasty chestnut soup. Then there is onion soup, another old French favourite made with a crust of toasted cheese croutons. The finely sliced onions are cooked slowly in butter for some thirty minutes, then sprinkled with flour which is allowed to brown before the water is added. The soup is then left to simmer for a further half-hour or so. The toasted croutons are floated on top of the soup, sprinkled with grated Gruyère and browned in the oven.

Onion soup, like *soupe à l'ail*, is strangely mild and soothing. For garlic soup peel a large quantity of cloves of garlic. Melt them in butter, season and then slowly add milk and stew gently for at least half an hour with a *bouquet garni*. Remove the *bouquet garni* and sieve the soup. This soup is generally served, like *garbure*, poured over some thin slices of stale bread.

For those who, like my late father, believe that soup is a meal in itself, there is always minestrone. The trouble with minestrone is that it comes in many fearful guises and can be as disgusting as any soup imaginable. A certain amount of trouble needs to be taken if it is to be made properly and then it can only be a treat.

Roughly chop the onions and melt them in olive oil with the garlic; add chopped carrots, celery and herbs. Add soaked flageolet beans and cover with water or stock. Bring to the boil and add French beans snapped in half. Simmer the minestrone for a good hour before adding the green vegetables which may be cabbage, peas, broccoli or spinach according to the season or your taste and cook for a further half-hour. Minestrone is especially good if a strong meat stock is used. And there can be no doubt that a good minestrone is a meal in itself.

Let me say one last word in praise of the French and their soups. One of their most brilliant inventions is a *bouillon de légumes* which they serve to those who have over-indulged or who have, for other reasons, trouble with their *foie*. Once you have had it you will yearn for it at the slightest sign of queasiness. It consists of the water in which an onion, a carrot, some cabbage, a leek, and a turnip if you like, have been cooked. As you gain strength and your normal appetite returns, gradually thicken your bouillon with a little potato.

By the time you have tried all these soups February which is a short month will have whistled by, the first snowdrops and aconites will have raised their courageous heads and, with luck, there will even be a promise of spring in the air. If the dreariness of the season has led you to drown your sorrows in over-indulgence you will be quietly enjoying your delicious *bouillon de légumes*, and adding a little more potato to it every day.

February Wines

The problem of what, if anything, to drink with soups takes on a new dimension if, in the straitened circumstances of our times, soup is the only nourishment offered – with bread – at an evening party for young people. These soup parties strike me as a much better idea than the wine-and-cheese parties with which the impecunious young used to entertain themselves. In my own young days these were given chiefly by nurses sharing flats together, usually up twenty flights of steps somewhere west of Olympia. Guests were expected to bring their own wine, which was sometimes poured together in a bowl with a single bottle of vodka supplied by the hostesses. The idea was to overcome the traditional sexual timidity of the English male and I suppose it worked, but the combination of foul wine and cheese wrought havoc on everyone's digestion. Nurses who looked incredibly appetising in their white starched aprons and black stockings never looked quite the same in floppy jerseys and trousers. Everybody's breath turned sour by the end of the evening; someone had invariably taken up permanent occupation of the only lavatory; someone else was sick. No doubt many successful marriages were made this way, but even at the time it seemed something of an obstacle course, like the traditional Catholic view of this world as a vale of tears preparing us for unimaginable delights hereafter. Such marriages were definitely not made in heaven.

For the soup party, assuming the soup to be either a thick vegetable soup in the French manner, or a chicken consommé with lumps of vegetable like cockie-leekie or minestrone, I would recommend a choice of Italian red and white wines. Young people show a marked preference for white wine at parties, which puzzles me since all but a few whites turn thin and sour after the third or fourth glass, but it is as well to cater for this preference, ordering two or three bottles of white to every one of red. The best white wine, when the purpose of drinking it is to become mildly intoxicated as inexpensively and painlessly as possible, should have a pronounced but bland taste with very little acid. Orvieto wine is too ambitious for this purpose, but there are some Tuscan whites available from Recount wines of Lower Sloane Street in the lower B price range which have a good strong taste of wine but little else – no identifiable fruit, no acid at all but plenty of alcohol and plenty of taste. My own choice, when entertaining a huge party of Durham University undergraduates, was for a Pinot Grigio from the Grave del Friuli, in north-east Italy. A vast amount was consumed, but there were no disgraceful scenes. For a red, I chose a Rioja Alberdi from Laymont and Shaw at the expensive end of the 'B' range, but if I had my life again I think I would serve the Chianti Putto from Recount at £2.50. This wine has the tremendous advantage, for a slurping wine, that one can drink vast quantities of it with none of the usual bad effects of a cheap wine, and it never changes its taste.

At my daughter's ball for the *jeunesse dorée* of Durham University they had much more to eat than soup, but I should imagine that the same considerations apply, *mutatis mutandis*, to these Supplementary Benefit or Youth Opportunities soup parties which are such an established feature of the February social scene. It is a great mistake to go for the cheapest wines in the A price range. Although, as I say, it is possible to find some acceptable wines in this range if one searches hard enough – like the Bulgarian merlot and cabernet sauvignon, the occasional *vinho verde* or mysteriously cheap Gewürztraminer – I would not care to drink too much of them at any one time. Blindness, lack of sensibility at the extremes and even paralysis can result.

Now let us forget about the young with all their problems and concentrate on Life as it really is. The problem with soup at a dinner party is that there is really very little one can usefully drink with it, but the English feel they have to be drinking something alcoholic throughout the permitted hours between six o'clock in the evening and bed-time after midnight. Sometimes people make the mistake of serving a light Mosel or Rhine wine in pretty green long-stemmed glasses. This may look very tasteful but I feel it provides altogether too much liquid. Different liquids of different temperatures travelling in succession down the oesophagus cannot be healthy. Most soups, especially the thick ones with a base of potato, lentil or split peas, are improved by a small glass of dry sherry. I do not think there is any wine to drink with bortsch, or onion soup, or garlic soup, and certainly none should be drunk with the *bouillon de légumes* recommended for moments of indigestion. Almost any wine is equally good with the meaty part of a *pot au feu* although I choose a clean, light red, like Bourgeuil or Thouarsais or Beaujolais at a pinch.

The problem of what to drink with a bouillabaisse has stumped greater men than I. As a general rule, I maintain that if you cannot make up your mind whether to drink white or red with a particular dish, it is not a rosé you are seeking so much as a quiet, unnoticed death. The idea that a rosé, because of its colour, is somehow half-way between red and white is utterly wrong. It is an idle host's way out of making a decision. But bouillabaisse is about the only dish with which I have always drunk rosé, chiefly for geographical reasons. The best bouillabaisse comes from Marseilles and the French Mediterranean coast between Toulon and the Spanish border, and the world's best rosé comes from Tavel (range D) or Lirac (range C), in the southern Rhône. There are no good whites from this area, or I have never discovered them, but there is another excellent rosé – so pale as to be called *gris de gris* – made by the huge Salins du Midi in the Camargue under the trade name Listel. This is considerably cheaper than Tavel, and can be bought in England from Les Amis du Vin in Shepherds Bush, but I find it does not taste so nice in England. This is not because of some mysterious failure to "travel" but because, in England, we all traditionally drink much better wine than we do in France. What tastes delicious on the beach or under the *pins parasols* of an elegant Provençal terrace seems pretty waterish, mass-produced stuff in England – which is what it is, I fear. So drink Listel *gris de gris* on the Mediterranean coast, Tavel or Lirac in England.

My wife's suggestions for a Valentine's Day dinner on February 14 raises several problems. No doubt she hopes to be given champagne. Champagne drinkers, in my experience, divide – often without knowing it – into those who prefer the *blanc de blancs* taste of wines made from the Chardonnay grape alone, or with a heavy pre-ponderance of the Chardonnay grape, and those who prefer the heavier *blanc de noirs* taste with a big element of *pinot noir* or, in the case of Krug, *pinot meunier*. My own favourite in the first range is Laurent-Perrier's "prestige" label, Cuvée du Grand Siècle, although the Pommerys are good, and a slightly cheaper *grande marque* which I generally keep in the house is Billecart-Salmon's non-vintage, available from Windrush wines of Cirencester. But my heart is really among the pinot wines. Best of all is Bollinger's RD 1975, followed by Krug. A good cheaper example of this style is Ayala, and cheapest of all something called De Telmont N.V. *brut* from Majestic Warehouses. That is in Range E, with Billecart-Salmon hovering between E and F. The others mentioned are GG.

But I am not sure I would serve champagne with the meal proposed by my wife for St Valentine's Day. I say that champagne goes with everything but there are certain foods – caviare is one, raw onions another and, to a lesser extent, egg – which go with no grape product at all. I suppose vodka would be the thing to drink with Guérain's *oeuf poule au caviare*, but that is a desperate remedy when one reflects that vodka has no taste; people drink it only to drown their sorrows or escape from the desperate horrors of socialism. Although lobster and champagne is a famous combination, I have a slight dread of it having been once told, quite untruthfully, that the two ingredients combine to form a deadly poison. In any case, I feel that the slight and subtle taste of a lobster is best brought out by a really rich and heavy white Burgundy – or, since expense is apparently no object on this occasion, one of the blockbuster Californian Chardonnays of which brilliant examples are available from Robert Mondavi, Joseph Phelps and the new Shafer vineyards, all in Napa Valley, all in Range G. Much cheaper and very nearly as good are some of the Australian Chardonnays, notably Rosemount Show Reserve and Brown Brothers, mostly Range E.

I should certainly not serve a Chambolle-Musigny les Amoureuses with sautéed hearts flambéed in brandy and mustard, as my dear wife romantically suggests. It is a beautiful wine, but its quality would be lost among all that brandy and mustard – especially if it was Drouhin's les Amoureuses which has recently been lighter than it should be. This wine is also villainously overpriced – largely, I suspect, because it is much sought after by rich Belgian businessmen on dirty weekends with their secretaries. I think I would serve a light claret with these sautéed hearts – possibly having put it into a Chambolle-Musigny bottle first. It is the thought which counts.

The only time I ate hot goat's cheese was in August, at Monsieur Daguin's famous establishment in Auch, south-west France. At the time I was drinking Madiran, a local red wine of no great interest, usually recommended to go with cassoulet (although I prefer an old Corbières). The reason I drank it was that Monsieur Daguin recommended it as a good local wine in Michelin. If owners of expensive restaurants recommend local wines, one will go for them every time since they are much cheaper than the prodigious prices one has to pay for classical wines. At any rate, the Madiran went very well with grilled goat's cheese, and I feel that I may have made a great discovery, except that very few wine merchants in Britain stock it. I notice that fewer and fewer heavily starred restaurants nowadays recommend local wines in their Michelin entries. It is a sad thing that expensive restaurants – in England too – tend to put such a huge mark-up on their better wines, because it means that unless one is prepared to double or triple the cost of the meal, one always drinks inferior wine in the best restaurants. This not only diminishes the sum of human happiness in the world; it also means that restaurateurs sell less good wine and probably attract less custom as a result. A few restaurants – like the Crown, Southwold – make a point of never adding more than £3 to the price of any bottle. As a result, they do a roaring trade. The only other restaurant I know which sells seriously good wine at reasonable prices is at the Tate Gallery in London. Both should be encouraged.

MARCH

The idea of having a picnic in a car-park is not an immediately attractive one. It conjures up strips of tarmac judiciously placed in otherwise unspoilt beauty spots where families with grannies sit on folding chairs munching sandwiches, supposedly admiring the countryside but more probably staring straight into the boots of their cars. Worse still are picnics in lay-bys where any hope of peace is shattered by the roar of long-distance lorries as they go thundering past laden with French cauliflowers or whatever.

But, before we scoff too readily at those who choose to picnic in such public places, perhaps we should consider, that, while the March winds are still whistling across the countryside, English families can be seen wrapped in their warmest and ugliest clothes and accompanied by their week-end guests picnicking on freezing hillsides at point-to-point meetings up and down the land. Later in the year they picnic in similar car-parks at Badminton, at Sandown or at Henley. The only positive advantage that I can see in such public places is that the picnicker can casually glance into the boot of his neighbour's car and see what he is eating.

Some people think that it is vulgar to be seen eating in public and, although I do not share this prejudice, I do think that it is quite entertaining to watch other people eating especially when they are dolled up to the nines for a smart social occasion and when with half their minds they are concentrating on their appearance or on spotting among the throng some long-lost acquaintance. Loud voices in public are horrible when they belong to one's family or close friends but when they hail from unknown neighbours in a car-park they can be very funny. In fact there is nothing more peculiar than the sight of a group of people determined to have fun.

The only time that I have ever had a picnic in a car-park at a smart race-meeting I was very young and deeply impressed by the champagne and smoked salmon and, if I remember rightly, caviare, with which my lavish hosts plied me. This, I thought, was the life – but now, of course, I have put away childish things, and know that there is more to life than caviare.

Nevertheless, eating is important and those who plan to take large hampers to point-to-points should consider with care what to include.

In my experience point-to-point courses are bitterly cold. People dressed in huskies boast of the natural beauty of various courses, but show me a man who can appreciate natural beauty when he is blue with cold and very hungry.

So take some hot soup in a thermos. I maintain that the best soups for such an occasion are strong meaty stocks such as duck soup or pheasant soup. One of the best meat soups is the *bouillon* from a *pot au feu* or from a *bollito misto*. *Bollito misto* is made with a boiling chicken, a tongue, a piece of gammon, a piece of brisket with herbs and vegetables all cooked slowly together. The resulting stock is utterly delicious.

After you have warmed yourself up with the soup, what could be more appetising than a game pie? Line a loose-bottomed cake tin with hot water pastry. For the pastry use $\frac{1}{4}$ pt. water and 3 ozs. lard to $\frac{1}{2}$ lb. of flour. Bring the water and lard to the boil, add immediately to the flour and mould into a paste. Keep part of the pastry aside for the lid. Partly bake the pastry case before filling with a mixture of game – pigeon, pheasant, venison, all previously cooked, boned and chopped. Fill with melted jelly made from the juices in which you have stewed the game and cover with the remainder of the pastry. Brush the top with beaten egg and make a hole in the centre. Cook in a fairly hot oven until the pastry has set. A little chopped boiled gammon and perhaps a hard-boiled egg are a good addition to the rich game mixture. When the pie is cooked allow it to cool before turning it out.

Apart from a game pie you could always take a pheasant or duck terrine or some big fat baps filled with scrambled or even fried eggs.

I suppose people usually take fruit for dessert on their picnics, but there is nothing very appealing about apples or bananas out of doors in the cold. I think that on a dull day I would prefer a piece of good, rich fruit cake.

Of course the whole picnic scene depends on whether or not you are the kind of person who owns a beautiful wicker basket complete with knives and forks. If you are you may be prepared to offer a more sophisticated pudding like creamed rice which is simply cold rice pudding mixed with very thick cream and a little finely grated lemon or orange peel. Otherwise, if you are eating in your fingers you might like to take some crystallized fruit and an orange tart.

For the orange tart, partially blind bake the shortcrust pastry and then fill the case with a well-beaten mixture of 2 oz. butter, 1 oz. sugar, 1 oz. flour and an egg with a little cream. Cook for a further 20 minutes

and when the tart is cool cover with very fine slices of unpeeled orange which you have blanched and then cooked gently in orange juice and sugar.

Of course, as spring fades into summer and the weather gets warmer, you will gradually be tempted to move on to more traditional picnic food of cucumber sandwiches and cold chicken.

Apart from icy picnics and an occasional early Easter, March does not have very many gastronomic associations. There is always the March Hare who attended the Mad Hatter's tea party but I rather suspect that that took place in June as I seem to remember something about white roses being painted red or vice versa. Of course in March the young lambs bound as to the tabor's sound but in the West Country they have been bounding since before Christmas and right through January. In any case I am not prepared to discuss the slaughter, cooking and eating of milk-fed lamb. I don't know very much about it and it seems cruel waste indeed.

But, when it comes to cooking a proper leg of lamb or mutton, I am full of opinions. For one thing I firmly believe that lamb has as much right as beef to be under-cooked and when I roast a leg or a shoulder I serve it very pink. This makes a total nonsense of the rule that beef should be cooked for fifteen minutes to the pound and fifteen minutes over and lamb or mutton for twenty minutes to the pound and twenty minutes over. A rule which must be ridiculous anyway as how can a long thin piece of fillet take the same amount of time to cook through as a great thick rolled rib? Recently I cooked a $2\frac{1}{2}$ lb. piece of fillet for no more than forty minutes and it was definitely rather over-done which was sad. Usually I find myself feeding larger numbers of people and therefore I rarely buy so small a joint.

As far as timing the cooking of a leg of lamb is concerned, I am afraid that I do it entirely by eye. I never cook a small leg for longer than an hour. In order to make the skin crisp, squeeze the juice of an orange over your mutton joint before putting it in the oven and, when the time comes to carve the leg, do it as the French do, in horizontal slices from right to left. This way you have thinner and large slices.

A mutton or lamb joint is delicious served with haricot beans or, at this time of year when vegetable gardens should be full of purple sprouting broccoli, serve your lamb with broccoli and hollandaise sauce.

I am about to denounce an emperor with no clothes. For several years now the shops have been filled with this Italian broccoli called "calabrese" and it appears to be having a great *succès d'estime*. For a while I believed that it must be the most delicious vegetable of all time until one day the light dawned and now I maintain that it has no taste at all and that the stalkier, small-flowered, purple sprouting broccoli from our English gardens is a hundred times better. There is something rather cocky and self-assertive about those great bold, green heads and it seems as though too much effort has been put into their appearance. Give me purple sprouting broccoli every time.

In any case broccoli is particularly good with roast meat and, to return to the subject of spring lamb, I must admit to being particularly lucky in that the sheep which graze our fields and the lambs that bound in them turn up regularly on our table or in our deep freeze, which means that we have more than our share of lamb.

I have never really understood why, when one buys a whole animal to put in the deep freeze, it does not come with its offal. More than that I cannot understand why so many English butchers dispose of the brains. I think that brains are exquisite and I can think of no better dish than poached brains with black butter. They can also be dipped in batter and deep fried although I think that they are rather too rich served like this. In Italy brains fried in batter are often serve as part of a *fritto misto* in which the other ingredients may include artichoke hearts, zucchini and veal escalope.

Some people, like my husband, can remember every meal they have ever eaten, where they ate it, who they ate it with, and what they ate and what they drank. I cannot remember this kind of thing although I do have a good memory for other perhaps more useful things – who knows? Nevertheless there are meals which stand out in one's mind as some sort of landmark. For instance I can remember a lunch of frogs' legs *à la provençale* followed by steak and chips and cream cheese which I had near Mâcon some twenty years ago. So can I remember a meal eaten at around the same time at a town called Verdun-sur-Doubs, a small town which is described in the Michelin green guide as being situated where the nonchalant Doubs joins the turbulent Saône. There I ate *saucisse à la creme* for the first time. But I also remember – and I cannot think why – a lunch given to me at least twenty years ago by a young French woman who was living in London at the time. The lunch was absolutely simple and totally unremarkable except for the fact that it tasted more delicious than most lunches. It consisted of grilled lamb cutlets accompanied by a dish of delicious potatoes or, more properly, a *gratin dauphinois* made with layers of sliced potatoes alternating with layers of grated Gruyère or Emmenthal, salt, and pepper and knobs of butter. A little milk is poured into the dish and the potatoes are cooked in the oven for three-quarters of an hour to an hour. On this occasion the potatoes were strongly flavoured with fresh thyme.

Two fine old favourites not to be forgotten and both made from mutton are of course Irish stew and what I have always called a Lancashire hot pot, the latter made from the remains of a joint and probably despised in many quarters as being "twice cooked meat". Layers of meat, sliced carrots, onions and potatoes are put in a dish, water or stock is added and the whole thing is put in the oven until the vegetables are heated through and the sliced potatoes on the top have formed a crust. A sprig of thyme or rosemary will not go amiss here, either. In fact, a genuine Lancashire hot pot is made from best end of neck and sliced potatoes. They are covered with sliced onions and a further layer of potatoes. Seasoning and stock is added, and the dish is cooked slowly for about 2 hours in the oven.

Another time when, in my opinion, twice cooked meat comes into its own is in cottage pie or shepherd's pie. I think, probably in the face of much opposition, that cottage pie is much nicer and far less greasy made with twice cooked meat than with fresh mince. This may well be because the mince sold in England is made from inferior fatty cuts.

The French version of a cottage or shepherd's pie is called *hachis parmentier* and is usually made with the remains of some beef from a *pot au feu*. A layer of mashed potato is placed on the bottom of a dish.

On top of this goes the minced meat which has been turned over in a pan with some onions melted in butter and some chopped tomatoes. Another layer of mashed potato is put on top of the meat and the whole thing is sprinkled with grated cheese before being put to brown in the oven. I have never come across an *hachis parmentier* made with mutton.

Neither, come to that, have I eaten particularly good lamb or mutton in France. We once took some English cousins to dinner with some French friends, and were given mutton with a very strong, tangy taste to it. I imagined a delightful lamb gambolling its way through life in the foothills of the Pyrenees as it stuffed itself with aromatic herbs. But as we drove away my cousin explained in disgust that what we had been eating was uncastrated ram. For days after that my cousin would occasionally turn green and exclaim in horror, "Uncastrated ram!" My visions of a sweetly gambolling lamb were quickly dispersed and I must admit that I have since come across the same tangy taste while eating *gigot* in France.

But I have not solved the problem of castrating. Who first discovered that lambs needed to be castrated in order to taste good? And why have the French not learned about it? This is particularly strange as many years ago when my eldest daughter was a baby I lived in France and employed as a baby sitter a delightful woman whose husband was a *chartreur*, or an *hongreur*. A *chartreur* or an *hongreur* is a castrater and it is my belief that this man, from nine o'clock on Monday mornings until six o'clock on Friday evenings, spent his time castrating. I wonder why he overlooked the lambs.

Be that as it may, there are endless excellent things to be done with our good English lamb; for instance, later in the year when the summer vegetables begin to appear, the breast can be used up in a *navarin*, the cutlets can be braised with onions and tomatoes, served cold with mint butter, marinated in olive oil with lemon juice and herbs, dipped in breadcrumbs and grilled – or they can be roast in a crown and served with mashed potatoes. Whatever you do with lamb, so long as it is castrated and not overcooked, I feel sure it will be appreciated.

If you live in the country you are likely to be even more thankful than the city dweller when the evenings begin to lengthen and you can at last forget the winter months. As the first daffodils begin to appear it even seems possible that Londoners may be tempted to the country for a week-end.

To my mind week-end meals inevitably fall into some kind of pattern. There is Friday dinner which should be surprising and welcoming, then Saturday lunch which seems to demand something more solid and basic. Perhaps Saturday dinner should be the most elegant meal of the week-end, then there is Sunday lunch which is always Sunday lunch. If your guests are still with you on Sunday evening, remember that that is traditionally the time when your non-existent cook is out so you can serve cold meat, spaghetti or scrambled eggs with impunity.

Years ago when I first moved out of London and friends came to stay for the week-end, I would spend two entire days cooking before they arrived. *Tempora mutantur et nos mutamur in illis.* I no longer have the time or perhaps the inclination for such slavery. Nevertheless there are things, like soup, which can easily be made in advance, thus preventing one from spending the entire week-end in the kitchen.

It is also undoubtedly a good idea to cook a stew and have it ready to be heated for Saturday lunch. There is not a stew in the world which does not improve with re-heating. So on Saturday lunch you have only to put your stew in the oven along with some potatoes to bake, make some salad, and your problems – for that meal at least – are over.

When your guests arrive on Friday evening they will probably have quarrelled in the car so they must be made to feel that the journey was worthwhile. So make a special effort over Friday dinner. On these occasions I often serve fish. For some reason it tends to be unexpected and is invariably appreciated.

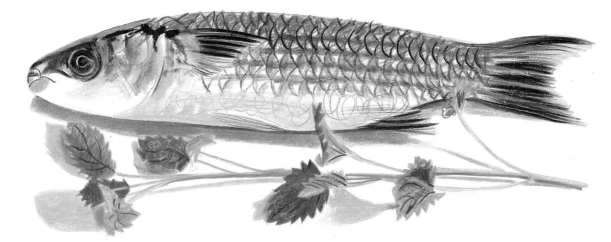

If you have doubts about fish – what to buy and how to cook it – invest in Alan Davidson's *Mediterranean Seafood*. He will tell you all you need to know. The book is admirably illustrated and a joy to read.

My fishmonger supplies some very fine grey mullet which I have lately taken to buying. The flesh is firm and succulent and, on the whole, people do not seem to be over-familiar with it. I wrap the seasoned fish in buttered tin-foil, having stuffed its belly with lemon balm, thyme, half a lemon and a lump of butter. Then I bake it slowly. The fish is delicious served with an hollandaise or mousseline sauce. If you plan to make an hollandaise sauce, please take the trouble to do it properly. It should not have the consistency of a béarnaise, but should come to the table light and frothy. A simpler sauce for fish is made from melted butter, lemon juice and chopped herbs – parsley, chervil or even tarragon.

It is not my habit to serve cheese at dinner during week-ends. After a light fish main course a pudding is more than welcome. What about the pancakes which I mentioned in February, filled with good quality strawberry jam and sprinkled with roasted almonds?

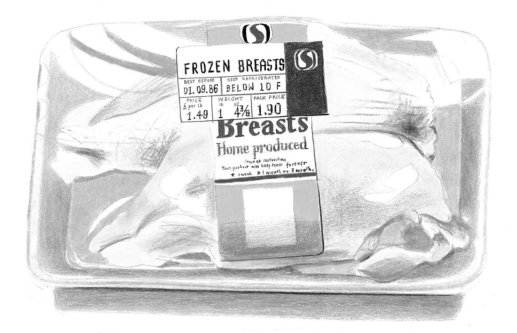

My reasons for not serving fruit at dinner are twofold. For one thing no one needs a three- or four-course meal twice a day. For another, when you are feeding the same people for a succession of meals, why not ring the changes with cheese and fruit at lunch and a pudding at dinner? Another piece of advice. If you have a selection of cheeses, do not put them all out at once. Keep some in reserve or your cheese board will look mangy and unappetising by the end of the week-end.

We have already dealt with Saturday lunch, but do not forget that instead of a stew a risotto may be ideal if you are feeding large numbers: the difference there being, of course, that a risotto cannot be made in advance. But it does have the blessed advantage of leaving only one pan to be washed up.

Week-ends are not really times for carefully prepared vegetables unless you have someone to help you in the kitchen. On Saturday evening you may serve something like a *suprême de volaille*. Nowadays most of the better supermarkets sell chicken breasts. Slice the breasts very finely and roll them in seasoned flour. Cook them in a pan in butter and when they are cooked remove to a heated dish. Pour cream into the pan and amalgamate it with the juices. Squeeze in some lemon juice and pour the sauce over the chicken. Serve with boiled rice and a green salad.

Sunday lunch looks after itself with a joint. If you fancy a first course you can provide a kipper pâté – or any other pâté for that matter, which you have made in advance. Equally, hard-boiled eggs stuffed with chopped anchovies and served with tomato salad make a tempting first course. Again, the eggs can be boiled beforehand and kept in the refrigerator.

You may feel that Sunday lunch is not Sunday lunch without a pudding. There was a wonderful period in my life when my daughter developed a passion for making treacle tart. Her talents were put to good use on many a Sunday, but, alas, she has now gone to London and I have reverted to simpler things like fruit salads or the now well-publicised mixture of cream and yoghurt. Equal quantities of cream and yoghurt are stirred together, covered with a thick layer of brown sugar and left for at least two hours in the refrigerator.

By Sunday evening you can relax and, whatever else may have happened, your guests will be delighted to have been freed from their own kitchens for a whole five meals.

March Wines

It is one of the great sorrows of my life that the chief author of this book refuses to countenance the idea of serving entire baby lambs, crisply roasted, at this time of year. With sucking pigs – similarly banned – they strike me as two of the most delicious foods which a Benign Creator has devised for our sojourn in this vale of tears. Both have been well known since the earliest times. The ban on roast sucking pig was imposed quite suddenly about twelve years ago, when we were eating it in a small restaurant in South-Western France at Easter and I foolishly said it reminded me of Alan Brien, the well-known journalist. The ban on milk-fed lambs has existed throughout the entire twenty-five years of our marriage. I attribute it to the fact that she was given subversive rubbish by the poet William Blake to read in the nursery. It may well be that her Anglican background leads her to be confused about the lamb's role at Easter. She should read Thomas Aquinas on this subject.

If ever she overcame her scruples, I would have no difficulty in choosing wines. With the milk lamb, we would quite simply drink whatever was the best bottle of old claret in my cellar at the time; with the sucking pig, whatever was my best bottle of old Burgundy.

Everybody – or nearly everybody – who has a wine cellar has at least one bottle which is so good – and nowadays so valuable – that he cannot bring himself to drink it. I have dozens and dozens of bottles which are so good that I cannot think of anyone I like enough for me to share them with. Another qualification must be that the person concerned likes his wine enough, otherwise one would be pouring the stuff down the throat of any visiting floozy who caught one's fancy and whom one wanted to impress. But the arrival of a milk lamb or a sucking pig would surely mark the occasion to bring out one's best, whether it was a Latour '45, a Cheval Blanc '47, a Margaux '53 . . . or, in the case of the pig, a hefty Vougeot '49 or one of the miraculous Nuits St George Roncières '69 still available from Avery's of Bristol at around £18 the bottle. The very best old Burgundy still available at the time of writing is probably Doudet Naudin's 1961 Beaune Clos du Roy available from Berry Bros at about £24 the bottle. Forget about Romanée-Conti and all the grotesquely over-priced *grands crus* which Americans fall over themselves to buy. This wine is as good as Burgundy can ever be, a most magnificent and beautiful wine. Looking at my own cellar, I think the only claret good enough which is still in ready supply also comes from Berry Bros, a 1966 Pomerol called Château Le Gay at £24 the bottle. But more remarkable single bottles can still be found if one shops around, notably on Avery's Special List of old wines in limited supply, and at Reid Wines, of Hallatrow, near Bristol.

But, instead of being asked to provide wine for such a feast in March or April, I am asked to recommend wines to drink with a cold chicken picnic in a car-park. The essence of picnic wines is that, except in moments of extreme heat (when one should offer a chilled Mosel Kabinett with plenty of chilled Perrier for those who are seriously thirsty), they should be red, strong, bland and instantly accessible. Almost any of the enormous variety of Côtes du Rhône available should fill the ticket. You do not want a "difficult" wine: it must be neither hard nor acidic; and must have plenty of taste to drown the metal drinking cups so often used on these occasions. It goes equally well with terrines, game pies, and makes the best of a bad job with scrambled egg baps.

Of the other dishes mentioned as being especially suitable for March, there is really nothing to be said about a roast leg of lamb, since any bottle of good red wine is a perfect accompaniment: the best of anything one can afford. I do not recommend, from the wine point of view, either mint sauce or red currant jelly, to be taken with your roast lamb. Those still old-fashioned enough to eat boiled mutton with an onion, egg or caper sauce will find it goes marvellously well with a young brute of a Châteauneuf, drunk at the year of production. Anything with a very creamy sauce (as opposed to béchamel, which should be the same, but isn't) presents problems for the serious wine drinker, since the creaminess can find itself in conflict with the richness of a heavy wine even to the point of making you feel queasy. I should recommend a young, light, cool, clean red from the Loire – possibly a red Sancerre of which the only good example I have found in England comes from Vacheron (Range D), or even a Beaujolais de l'Année (Range C). *Saucisse à la creme* is a little different owing to all the spices involved. There I would go really heavy, possibly to my beloved Château Musar if I was feeling poor, to an old Hermitage, if I was feeling rich. Irish stew, again, calls for a light red wine if not quite as light as the two listed above. Try a Bourgeuil or a Chinon.

I have never been able to eat Lancashire hot pot from twice cooked meat – in the days when English people had servants, it was a large part, if not the major part, of their function to finish off roast joints in this way – and don't much care for it when properly made with raw meat, either. This might be a time to drink beer – which was quite a normal lunchtime drink in respectable houses when I was a boy. Perhaps, in accordance with the spirit of the times – we are all drunker nowadays, and have less to do in the afternoons – it should be a strong ale, like Carlsberg's Special Brew. Cottage pie (made with raw mince) is, with risotto, one of the classic food vehicles for seriously good red wine, as well as being perfectly well accompanied by any red wine you like to drink. Nothing interferes with one's pleasure in the wine so long as one goes easy on the Worcester sauce and resists the temptation to add chutney. If your wife insists on using twice-cooked meat, either for cottage pie or for the less good shepherd's pie, I should plead an urgent engagement and eat elsewhere. *Hachis parmentier*, as my wife rather grandly calls her special cottage pie, should be drowned in Worcester sauce (but not, please, tomato ketchup) and accompanied by a red Côtes du Rhône or one of the cleaner, lighter Riojas in Range C.

For the March weekend house party which my wife has somewhat cursorily sketched, I would inevitably serve a white wine with Friday dinner. At the moment, we are drinking practically no white wines except the splendid 1983 Mâcon-Villages, and so long as they last we will probably drink nothing else. Sauvignon is too sharp to be welcoming for nervous guests. Really prized guests might score the 1983 Meursault from Dupont, but one does not want to drink too much of that too soon. The best of all the 1983 Mâcon-Villages I discovered – and nearly all are wonderful – was a Mâcon-Viré from Bonhomme sold by David Stevens at Grape Ideas, Oxford, and long since sold out. People arriving on Friday evening are usually in a state of some exhaustion and will not wish to be made too drunk, so no port or brandy. The suggested March pudding of pancakes plus strawberry jam would destroy most Sauternes, although a light one, like Doisy-Daene's noticeably clean 1978 (G) would probably win through by virtue of its purity. I think I would serve one of the joke dessert wines, like a Beaumes de Venise, whose *muscat* tastes like the concentrated essence of a muscatel dessert grape, which is what it is. This delicious wine is also highly alcoholic, and should send guests to bed. There are many excellent small Muscats de Beaumes de Venise, including a memorable one from the Beau-castel property sold by Bibendum of Regents Park Road, but the best (and most expensive) one readily available comes from Vidal Fleury. Cheaper and just as good – but harder to find – is the 1978 moscatel made by J. Fonseca in Setubal, Portugal, and generally known in the trade simply as Setubal. Colin Price-Beech, of Recount Wines, sometimes stocks it.

Saturday lunch – a stew, sometimes mysteriously dignified by the name of casserole – should be accompanied either by an old, heavy and complicated Châteauneuf or a young, light Burgundy, depending on the weather and the general mood. I have already discussed the difficulty of finding old Châteauneufs. Odd parcels turn up, if you keep your nose to the catalogues – the Wine Society, in Stevenage, suddenly produced a beautiful 1967 Mont-Redon a few years ago – but the real lesson about all these wines from the Rhône which need keeping is to lay them down, lay them down. There are many, good, light 1982 village or house Burgundies around. The best I found were a housewine called Geisweiler Cuvée 18me siècle from Peter Dominic at £3.80 and a village wine from somewhere called Coulanges Les Vineuses, in the north Burgundy region called Auxerrois, shipped by Morgan Furze at £3.86.

Saturday dinner, where elegance is the keynote, will send us mincing round our claret bins again, but if a *suprême de volaille* is planned I should produce a grand-sounding rather light one against the cream: Château La Lagune 1972 perhaps. The vintage was a wash-out in

Bordeaux, but Berry Bros. still have large stocks of nearly all the famous châteaux at give-away prices. None of them is too bad and some, like the La Lagune, are very good. For Sunday lunch I would produce a good bottle of Burgundy – either one of Avery's 1976 declassifieds or something grander, depending on the guests' rating (in terms of their joy and knowledge of wine, as well as the affection in which they are held). Don't serve Burgundy with kipper pâté, however. Personally, I feel it is vulgar and a little heavy-handed to have two table wines at lunch (not counting pudding wines at the end) and would probably suggest only sherry with kipper pâté. Sunday's dinner would be back to red Côtes du Rhone and Chianti, unless the guests were particularly keen on wine, when I would produce another good Burgundy, preferably a different one.

APRIL

However cold and rainy the weather may be in April, we have to face up to the fact that spring is at last here.

Some English people have a pathetically optimistic attitude to the seasons and what I regard as a peculiar way of acknowledging them. A ray of spring sunshine appears and they decide that winter is a thing of the past and begin to strip frantically. I am amazed by the numbers of near naked bodies to be seen in my local town of Taunton whenever there is a sunny day. Sometimes, in early spring, white arms, backs and thighs are pimply with cold and later in the mere two days of unusual sunshine the same arms, thighs and backs are to be seen smarting from sunburn, painfully red and blistered. I have never understood why people wish to expose their bodies in this uncomfortable way to the fumes of every passing car and to the disapproving eyes of the more old-fashioned shoppers. If it is in order to attract the opposite sex which is, I suppose, a possibility, then I can only marvel at the members of the opposite sex – whichever one – who succumb.

And yet I must admit to having a faint inkling as to what is going through the minds of these eager strippers, and, although I do not take off my clothes at the first sign of spring, I do begin to think in terms of different types of food. Fruit salad in place of roly-poly pudding – or roast chicken in place of cassoulet.

Now it is a great shame about chicken in England because it is rarely as nice as it should be and because it is almost impossible – unless you have your own chickens – to find a boiling fowl. I know that it is now possible in supermarkets in London – and probably in other large towns – to find the yellow, continental type of chicken which has been reared on grain. To listen to some people talking these days, you would think that the Kingdom of Heaven was to be found in Waitrose in the King's Road. Unfortunately we cannot all go to the Kingdom of Heaven and there are butchers and grocers all over the country selling your average white-skinned English chicken. And some of these white chickens even come without their giblets – and how, without giblets, are you supposed to make proper gravy?

If you are lucky enough to be able to find a real old-fashioned boiling fowl, you may be tempted to treat your Easter guests to a *poule au riz à la crème* which is an old favourite of mine, but one which, alas,

I rarely have the opportunity to make. Cook your chicken gently in fat with sliced carrots and onions, add stock and water, garlic and herbs. Bring to the boil, cover the pan and cook slowly in the oven for two to three hours. Before the chicken has finished cooking remove some of the liquid. Put the partly boiled rice and the stock in an earthernware dish in the oven and leave it there to finish cooking. Twice the volume of chicken stock to rice should be used. Meanwhile make the sauce with a roux and some of the chicken liquid. Whip in the yolks of two eggs off the heat before adding the cream. Stir in some chopped tarragon, carve the chicken and serve with the sauce poured over it.

There are various different ways in which an ordinary chicken can be treated if you don't want just to roast it. You can joint it and brown it in oil before gently cooking it in a little white wine with tomatoes, garlic, basil and black olives *à la provençale*. This is as good a way as any of treating an indifferent bird.

One way I particularly like chicken is in a *bollito misto*. I have already referred to this magical dish and I cannot recommend it too highly, particularly if you have large numbers to feed. First and foremost it is completely delicious, secondly one doesn't seem to come across it all that often, in this country at any rate, and lastly – a point by no means to be laughed at – the meat and all the vegetables are cooked in one huge pot which saves washing up.

You need a chicken, a piece of gammon, a piece of brisket and, if you are really going to town, an unsalted tongue. Most butchers in England have a strange habit of salting tongues almost automatically, so you may have some difficulty in finding a fresh one. Cover the meat in water, add a bouquet garni and a couple of cloves of garlic and bring to the boil. As the morning progresses add the vegetables according to the length of time which they take to cook. Carrots, turnips, leeks, whole onions, celery and potatoes. Serve your *bollito misto* hot on a huge dish with an accompaniment of vinaigrette to which you have added a couple of chopped hard-boiled eggs and some chopped herbs of your choice or with a thick tomato sauce. I think I prefer *bollito misto* served with the vinaigrette sauce but, whichever sauce you choose, make sure that there is enough of it.

Nowadays the supermarkets are full of chicken pieces – thighs, drumsticks and so forth with which various enjoyable things can be done. Soften some butter with a wooden spoon and beat in some Dijon mustard, a little Worcester sauce, some crushed garlic, salt and pepper and a pinch of garam masala and various spices. Coat the drumsticks

in the butter mixture and grill them. In any case there is no doubt that these slightly insipid pieces of meat profit from being cooked with garlic and spices.

Sometimes I cook drumsticks in a wok with a little sesame oil, ginger, garlic, leeks, spring greens, possibly a red pepper and a touch of soy sauce. This makes a change and goes down especially well with young persons.

If your thoughts turn to turkey as Easter approaches, I suggest a very simple stuffing made from the minced liver of the bird, some white breadcrumbs, a crushed clove of garlic, salt and pepper, some thyme and a beaten egg. I first ate this stuffing, made for a boiling fowl by an old lady in the South of France and was then, and still am now, amazed by its simplicity.

The more sophisticated among us have a tendency to forget one of the most wonderful of all sauces to be served with chicken or turkey. Let the *parlez-vous* laugh their heads off, but let us never forget the glories of bread sauce. To the initiated it is as hard to resist as mayonnaise or hollandaise or any of the more refined products of the best French kitchen. I have on occasion persuaded French people to try it, but the very idea of *sauce au pain* seems to arouse in them the same kind of disgust that some Anglo-Saxons will evince at the mention of frogs' legs or snails. But, just because you like bread sauce, do not think that thick gravy is all right too. Some people will react even more violently to thick gravy than to the idea of eating worms. I once knew a young West Country boy who calmly assumed that if the French ate frogs and snails they would be bound to offer him worms when he went to France. He appeared to be totally unmoved by the idea although I must admit that a faint smile of what seemed like relief crossed his face when I disabused him.

On the other hand, the father of a friend of mine turns green at the mention of thick gravy because it reminds him of the gravy served thirty years ago in a hotel in Rugby where he used to go when taking his son out from school. The son, it must be added, was the one who ate the thick gravy, the father merely had to watch.

The nastiest gravy that I can remember was, not surprisingly, school gravy which used to be poured like custard, from a large white jug over one's food and which formed a skin as soon as it touched the plate. Happily there is no need to dwell for long on such unpleasant things.

Partly because it is cheap and partly, perhaps, because no one ever seriously dislikes it, chicken tends to be eaten rather a lot whereas duck, on the other hand, is much less frequently served – in England at any rate. But in France duck is on the up and up. It is amazing how high a proportion of starred restaurants in the Michelin guide list *foie de canard*, *magret de canard* or *aiguillettes de canard* among their specialities these days. I happen to have a 1974 Michelin guide and glancing through it recently I found that not one of twenty starred restaurants which I chose at random listed duck at all.

The great boom area is in *magret de canard* for which the duck are especially bred. The breast is removed whole and treated and served very much as though it were steak. In fact it often tastes almost indistinguishable from steak which is rather a shame, I think.

In *La Cuisine en 20 Leçons*, an excellent book which deals with most of the favourite French dishes in the clearest and most straightforward way, Pellaprat gives as good a recipe for *Canard à l'orange* as you are likely to find. Brown the duck in butter, drain off the fat and add some already prepared *sauce brune* (or demi-glace), season with salt and add the finely peeled skin of two oranges. Cover the pan and leave the duck to cook for some forty-five minutes. Meanwhile peel two more oranges. Slice the peel very finely and blanch it for three minutes in boiling water. Slice finely the four oranges, making sure that no pith or pips remain. When the duck is cooked skim the fat off the sauce and strain the sauce. Add the bleached sliced skins, the juice of an orange, $\frac{1}{2}$ a teaspoonful of sugar and a tablespoonful of Curaçao. Carve the duck and serve it with the sauce poured over it and decorated with the sliced oranges, some *pommes parisiennes* and a green salad.

One reason why people may hesitate to buy duck when their friends come, is that there is surprisingly little meat on a duck and one bird will only feed four people unless it is carved by a Chinaman. We sometimes buy a *canard lacqué* in Soho and take it home to find that a *canard lacqué* carved by a Chinaman is not unlike the contents of a Leprechaun's purse. So long as you don't look away, there seems to be an endless supply. Another disadvantage to duck is, of course, the amount of fat it produces. But with care the fat can be removed and if preserved it is excellent for cooking with.

In any case it is rather a shame that we don't cook duck more often as there are many ways of cooking it besides *à l'orange*, most of which are simple and all of which are delicious. Besides, guests like duck because they feel they are being given a treat and that an effort has been made on their behalf.

For a *canard aux olives*, make a stuffing with the liver, a handful of chopped, stoned green olives, some breadcrumbs soaked in milk, salt, pepper and a beaten egg. Brown the duck in a little butter and allow the fat to run. Pour off the fat and *flambé* the duck in Cognac or Marc de Bourgogne. Add half a glass of white wine, cover the pan and allow the duck to cool gently in its own juices for about three quarters of an hour. Add some whole, stoned green olives to the pan before serving.

Duck is equally delicious cooked with turnips or peas or celery, or roast in the traditional English way with apple sauce, apple sauce being one of the great delights of this world.

One of the most memorable ducks I have ever eaten was, needless to say, in Paris and also, needless to say, in a Chinese restaurant. There were six of us – Bron, myself and four French friends – and we had spent an entire week-end gourmandising. By Sunday evening we really had no need of another morsel but when dinner time came round we began to wonder what to do. It was finally decided that, as we had had so much to eat over the last couple of days, what we really needed was a change. No straightforward bistro would do. We had no appetite left for traditional French food. The obvious thing to do was to go to a Chinese restaurant to eat a Pekin duck. So first we had the glorious, crispy skin which we wrapped with some plum jam and a spring onion in a little pancake. When we had gorged ourselves silly on these small parcels the main course came. The main course consisted of the flesh of the duck – and we were off again. Almost as much as the exquisite taste of the duck itself, I remember how much we laughed. We laughed and we laughed and we were mainly laughing quite simply from over-eating.

When one thinks of Chinese cooking and duck in Chinese restaurants one inevitably thinks of duck with ginger. In his *Complete Chinese Cook Book*, Kenneth Lo gives several delicious duck recipes – most of which require ginger, including an especially good one for "quick fried ribbon of duck with shredded ginger". Sliced root ginger, chilli peppers, soaked black beans, sliced celery, leeks and a sweet pepper, garlic and sliced roast duck meat are all cooked quickly in hot fat and seasoned with soya sauce, sugar and ginger.

If you are lucky you may have not just a duck but a goose for your Easter lunch. We used to keep geese on our pond where we mistakenly supposed they would eat the weed. We acquired them in exchange for some port from a neighbour and soon grew so fond of them that although they failed to eat the weed we could not bring ourselves to eat them. They bred and bred so that there was soon a great flock of them. They earned their keep, we maintained, as watchdogs. One day, after several years, as I drove out to go shopping there was a bump and a terrible crunch and one poor ancient goose bit the dust. I wept great tears and to the intense fury of my family refused to eat the bird. One of my sisters-in-law who was then living near-by was quite rightly infuriated by the waste and took the bird away to put in her deep freeze. At a later date she invited us to eat it. Never ever can there have been a tougher goose. My poor sister-in-law had done all she could but there was no doubt about it that the bird was too old.

I have since learned that ideally a goose should never weigh more than about eight pounds and only young birds aged between four and six months should ever be eaten. I am not surprised.

When roasting your young goose place it on a grill in the roasting dish so as to allow the fat to be drained off more easily.

Of course one of the best things about a goose or even a duck is the liver. There can be no more delicate taste than the taste of fresh goose or duck liver.

Although nowadays trout, like strawberries, are available all the year round, it is still the case that salmon trout at any rate are at their best from April until July and so you might well at Easter time and with the advent of spring decide to turn your back on the usual Easter bird and serve trout.

Only recently the man with whom I have shared my life for the last twenty-four years and who, for all that time, has been content to start his day with a mere cup of coffee, awoke with the bright idea that what we really needed was a tank in the kitchen out of which we could fish trout and crayfish for our breakfast. The idea was not welcomed wholeheartedly, but it occurred to me that the trout fishing season was upon us and a fishing rod lay idle in the hall so he might well have liked to rise early and set out like primitive man to catch the family breakfast. A stream runs through our village in which local boys often catch beautiful trout. What need have we of a tank in the kitchen?

Tanks and fish farms are in fact cropping up all over the place and it is becoming increasingly easy to buy large fat Rainbow trout at any time. Some maintain that these fish are not so good as river trout, but they can, in my opinion, be quite delicious.

The arcane laws of British sportsmanship which lead us to suppose ourselves to be the most "gentlemanly" people in Europe, dictate, I believe, that fishermen should throw small trout straight back into the river from which they came. A French restaurateur once stayed with us. He cooked exquisite meals in the evening and during the day went "hunting". One day he returned with two pheasants-out-of-season, a squirrel, a fox and a songbird. The next day he returned with a miraculous draught of titchy trout. We threw up our hands in dismay, horrified to see so many young lives nipped in the bud, but that night we dried our eyes and ate the fish.

Larousse Gastronomique gives a recipe for trout which might lead one to think that fishing had never been a sport, but always a matter of tanks in the kitchen. "Ten minutes before serving, take the fish out of the water, despatch them with a blow on the head," it reads. I have another French cookery book which urges me to seize a living trout by the tail, to beat it to death on a table and to gut it instantly through the gills. So, if you have no tank, you should clearly take a table and your *batterie de cuisine* fishing with you.

Quite apart from all that, there is no doubt about it that a fresh trout – rainbow or river – is an excellent fish to be treated with care if its quality is to be fully appreciated.

Opinions differ as to whether it is better to poach your fish in a *court-bouillon* or in water. Personally I do not see the advantage of a *court-bouillon* since a fresh trout should be able to stand on its own merit. In the absence of a fish kettle, trout – or salmon for that matter – can be wrapped in buttered silver foil and baked in a medium oven. Season the fish first and place a lump of butter, a slice of lemon, some fennel or lemon balm in the belly. When you take the fish out of the oven only partly unwrap it so that you can test that it is cooked by inserting a sharp knife along the backbone.

To my mind *truite aux amandes* is a recipe best left to restaurants, and one which, in any case, is highly over-rated.

Trout should be accompanied by only the lightest and most delicate of sauces such as an hollandaise or *sauce verte*. For a *sauce verte* add blanched and pounded spinach, watercress, tarragon and parsley to your hollandaise. Or you may serve a *sauce mousseline*. If your trout is to be cold, the obvious sauce is a mayonnaise. Watercress and spinach can likewise be added to mayonnaise. If anything, they make it slightly less rich. Although it is not strictly correct, the watercress and spinach need not be blanched for a mayonnaise, so long as they are very fresh and finely chopped.

Louisette Bertholle in *French Cooking for All* gives an excellent recipe for trout in aspic.

It is important to take care what vegetables you serve with fish. Boiled or steamed potatoes are *de rigueur* with trout. Nothing else can take their place. I would serve a green salad separately – watercress if you haven't used it in your sauce, or cucumber. Tomatoes won't be welcome but a salad of French beans might. And, whatever you do, don't forget to eat the cheek.

April Wines

Chicken, duck and trout seem to be the main theme for entertaining over the Easter period. I remember when chicken was a tremendous treat. In those days – I am talking about the years immediately after the war, when everything was mysteriously in short supply and the politicians had the time of their lives, directing us all left, right and centre – roast chicken always came with a stuffing *and* bread sauce. At my prep school, any boy who was taken out by his parents for Sunday luncheon and could not truthfully say that he had been given chicken at the local hotel invariably told a lie. To have eaten anything else involved tremendous loss of face. Such things as steak were unknown, at any rate until one reached public school. Many people had chicken with their Christmas lunch. Personally, I feel there are few things as good as a fat, grain-fed roast capon, but these are almost unprocurable nowadays, and it may be in deference to the ambiguous nature of roasting fowl sold in the big chain stores, most of which have been fed on fish-meal and taste of it, that people often decided to serve a rosé wine with it. Perhaps they are uncertain nowadays whether fowl counts as fish or meat. In fact almost any wine goes with roast chicken, but I should not serve a rosé with it for fear of revealing your innermost doubts and anxieties. As I may have suggested already, I am generally against the serving of rosé in England. They are seldom very good wines with the exceptions of Tavel, Lirac and the almost unprocurable Marsannay, from the very north of Burgundy near Dijon, and in any case are better drunk in their region of production. There is no good reason for drinking them in England.

Because roast chicken is now so plentiful and cheap, as well as being easy to cook for the new generation of idle, unfulfilled housewives, one needs to up-grade the wine served with it, or guests will feel they are being short-changed. As I say, any wine goes well with chicken, but make it expensive. The same is true of boiled chicken, which is a perfect vehicle for any heavy red wine, whether French, Italian, Californian or Australian. It might be a good time to experiment with new wines, like a Zinfandel from California (the best dry Zinfandel I have yet discovered was also extraordinarily cheap, the 1979 from Wente Brothers) which I like but by no means everybody else does, or some of the Chilean Cabernets which are beginning to arrive here. When boiled chicken is served in its most exquisite form, a *poule au riz à la crème*, one can only do what the people of Bourg-en-Bresse do and bring out one's best old Burgundy. Others maintain this is the ideal time to drink an auslese from the Rhine or a *vendage tardive* riesling from the Alsace – even some of the semi-sweet wines of Anjou and the central Loire grown from the chenin blanc grape. Well, let them say so, but if anyone served a *poule au riz à la crème* to me with a Vouvray moelleux, I would scream.

Little bits of chicken, sold in pieces and cooked with clever spicy sauces, are best served with clever, spicy little wines like Retsina, which is very cheap indeed in Range B, or Alsatian Gewürztraminer, of which mysteriously cheap examples can sometimes be found but are generally in Range C. Turkey is such an uninteresting bird that again, unless the dear little wife has really exerted herself over a miraculous stuffing, one must try to be interesting with the wine: something rich, powerful and unusual, like a very old Cornas or Bandol would be ideal. Otherwise ask your grocer for his best Zinfandel and watch their faces as they drink it.

Reference is made in the main text to eating worms, but as I have never knowingly eaten them I cannot say which wine might be best. Champagne, as I say, goes with nearly everything. Ducks, which are famous for eating worms, may be served with any red wine, the better the wine the happier everyone will be. Smart alecks suggest serving spätlesen from the Rhine with duck, and no doubt that is what one would drink in Germany, but I can see no possible reason for doing any such thing so long as good, strong red wine is available. Perhaps in the special circumstances of a Pekin duck, when one eats the skin first within a small pancake with plum jam and spring onion, there might be a case for drinking a German wine with the first course. I feel it would be a trifle precious and self-conscious; in any case, one generally eats Pekin duck in a Chinese restaurant, whose wine lists are nearly always pretty appalling. I have a peculiar habit when it comes to Chinese food, always drinking a medium white Graves with it. This is not a wine I would dream of drinking with anything else and I quite accept that it is somewhat insulting to lump all Chinese food together as if it were a single entity, instead of being composed of as many ingredients as European food – if not more of them. Yet the fact remains that, whether I am eating duck with ginger, crab with ginger, sliced beef in oyster sauce, prawns with red pepper or sweet and sour pork, I always drink this same wine which is something I would never have with anything else. My reason is partly that it is cheap, partly that there are seldom any good wines on the list, but chiefly that in a Chinese restaurant one is generally eating an extraordinary mixture of fish, meat and fowl with many different sauces, some quite highly spiced, and this is the only wine I have discovered which is bland and non-reactive enough to ride them all. In the case of home cooking, out of a wok, one tends towards single dishes and in any case never has a bottle of medium Graves in the house, so other considerations apply. Depending on whether fish or meat predominates, I would probably choose a Gewürztraminer or a Bourgueil.

The same considerations apply for goose as for duck, although I have heard people say that the best thing to drink with goose is sweet, strong cider, possibly laced with applejack or calvados. However, as I have never tried out this bizarre idea, it would be unkind to recommend it. My great objection to cider and beer is that they are not strong enough, and although they might serve to quench the thirst at lunch on a working day, they are basically a waste of good drinking space. Strong ales can now be found in abundance, but even the strongest ciders are not strong enough for my tastes.

Trout is such a delicate fish that almost any wine drowns it. Its trouble is that it has two separate tastes – the skin, which could carry quite a hefty spätlese, even a light white chardonnay, and the flesh, whose subtlety is threatened even by the lightest and most flowery Mosel. As I am not too keen on swopping between riesling-based and classic French grapes in the course of a single meal, and as a trout seldom constitutes more than a single course, at any rate when one has guests, I tend to serve no wine at all with trout.

The important subject of goose and duck livers has been left for another chapter, but at this point I would like to put in a little protest against the growing habit, which we have caught from France, of serving these delightful substances with a sweet dessert wine. There are those nowadays who maintain that the exquisite wines of Sauternes and Barsac should be served with nothing else. I should like to put in an early word here, in case anyone plans a foie gras treat for Easter and wonders whether to be fashionable and serve their best Château d'Yquem at the same time: **don't do it**. For the present, stick to champagne with your foie gras.

MAY

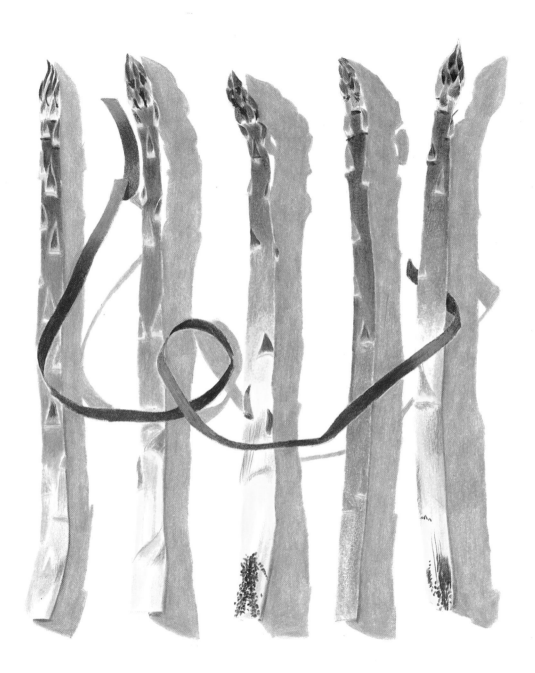

The first summer vegetables, like the first snowdrops and the first cuckoo, never fail to delight and even the most pessimistic of us must feel a surge of optimism at the sight of fresh peas and baby carrots – both of which begin to appear in the shops in May.

French people find the thought of English green peas almost as funny as they find the idea of eating jam with meat. I tend to share their opinion on red-currant jelly and lamb, but they are undeniably mistaken about our peas. Frozen peas as big as marbles, served as they generally are in pubs with steak and fish and chips, are totally unacceptable. But peas in England are not always like that. It is interesting to note that the French boil their peas for at least twenty minutes even when they cook them in the "English" way. I am sure, however, that most people will agree that there is nothing more tempting than small, fresh, lightly boiled green peas with butter and mint – mint is one of the few herbs which is rarely used in French cooking.

But, when the peas are larger and a little older, they are undoubtedly better when cooked *à la francaise*. An onion should be melted in butter, then the peas are added with several chopped lettuce leaves, salt, pepper and a little sugar. Cover the peas with water and stew for a good half an hour. Do not drain, but serve with the juice. Some chopped bacon melted with the onion is a good addition.

Peas are also an essential ingredient of a *navarin à la printanière* – a delicious lamb stew to which any fresh, young vegetables can be added. The rather powdery consistency of peas helps to thicken the gravy of a *navarin*.

As the summer really comes into its own, people will be asking each other whether they prefer raspberries or strawberries, but in May they are still undecided on the pea/broad bean dilemma.

One thing about broad beans is that they are, perhaps, a little more adaptable than peas. They can be served hot with cream and chopped parsley as a first course – if they are large it is better to remove the outer skins. Or they can be served – as indeed they frequently are – tossed in butter with bacon. They are excellent as part of an *hors d'oeuvre* – raw, skinned and sprinkled with salt.

Broad beans, like peas, make a wonderful addition to a *navarin*.

Perhaps everybody knows by now about *salade dite chaude* which can be made with lettuces but which is particularly delicious with fresh young spinach leaves. It makes an ideal first course. To the salad made in the usual way add croutons of fried bread, fried, chopped bacon and chicken livers. Pour the juices from the bacon and the chicken livers over the salad. This is really only a more sophisticated version of the old French favourite *salade de pissenlit* made from young dandelions and bacon.

I wonder whose idea it was to go gathering nuts in May. They cannot have had a great deal of success and should perhaps have turned their thoughts to lettuces, radishes or globe artichokes instead. The very thought of the month of May is uplifting with its lilac, lambs, laburnum and even an early rose *"en sa belle jeunesse, en sa première fleur"* – but no nuts. In fact there are very few vegetables to be found in the garden yet at this time of year in England.

But Globe artichokes do appear early in the summer. I prefer the small, purplish Italian variety to the big, fat French ones. But in either case they can be served hot with melted cream instead of butter for a change. They eat them like this in Normandy although in most parts of France artichokes – like asparagus – are usually served cold with vinaigrette. Should you wish to use only the *fonds*, then, of course, it is advisable to buy the large French artichokes.

It is really rather surprising what little use we make of artichokes in this country since they grow here very easily and because of their arrival on the scene so early in the season must be welcome.

Artichokes are among the commonest and cheapest vegetables in Italy and so it is hardly surprising that the Italians have discovered many delicious ways of cooking them. I particularly like them *alla veneziana*. The small dark artichokes are used for this. The outer leaves are removed and the artichokes are slowly simmered in a mixture of olive oil, stock and white wine with a sprig of rosemary.

Sliced artichokes fried in batter are so good that it is astonishing that they only ever seem to be found in Italy where, as I have said, they often form part of a *fritto misto*.

But the French too have some excellent ways of preparing artichokes which seem to be somewhat overlooked elsewhere.

There appears to be some disagreement as to the correct way of cooking *artichauts à la barigoule*, but basically the artichokes which have had their ends cut off and their outside leaves removed are boiled in salted water for about ten minutes. Then the leaves are opened out,

the choke is removed and the centre of the artichoke is filled with a mixture of chopped ham, onion, garlic and parsley. The artichokes are then tied up and stewed gently in a little olive oil and white wine in a covered pan for about an hour. Some people add a little tomato purée – or perhaps a couple of peeled, chopped tomatoes – to the wine and oil.

Artichokes cooked this way make a good and rather unusual first course for a dinner party.

Because they tend to go in for the larger pale artichokes, the French also have many good recipes for the *fonds*. The first time I remember eating *fonds* was in Paris when I was about sixteen. They were served in a traditional way as a accompaniment to a *rôti de boeuf* with a béarnaise sauce and I remember that meal as an important contributory factor to the blind love of France which I was fast developing at around that time. Francophiles may well talk of French literature – French history – the French countryside – the châteaux of the Loire – the tree-lined roads – the exquisite precision of the language, but what really wins their hearts is the smell of France, the first *steak et frites* which they eat, on arriving, and the occasional *rôti de boeuf béarnaise* with *fonds d'artichaut.*

I sometimes wonder about the opposite. What it is that Frenchmen love about England? And there is no doubt that a great many French people do love England. A close French friend of mine who has a somewhat romantic attachment to England seems to love the rain. He once came to stay and when he arrived, to my delight, the sun was shining and the garden looking at its English best. The following morning there was a heavy grey sky and a dull drizzle permeated everything. A beatific smile spread across my friend's face as he drew a deep breath and said: *"Ah, maintenant je suis en Angleterre!"*

To return to artichoke hearts. Besides being served as a plain accompaniment to roast beef, they may be stuffed with a variety of different things such as spinach, mushrooms in béchamel, stewed tomatoes, a purée of peas or minced ham in béchamel. In these cases sprinkle with grated Gruyère and heat the *fonds* in the oven until the cheese on top has browned.

Asparagus does not usually appear quite so early as artichokes do and you may even have to wait until June for it to be ready in your garden, although not invariably. But by May it is bound to be in the shops. I may, in my time, have bought artichoke hearts in jars but I cannot for the life of me imagine who would buy tinned asparagus. It is invariably disgusting and, although I must admit to having used the frozen variety in a tart, I would advise people who can't find fresh asparagus to go without it. Asparagus, like new potatoes, can only really be eaten in season which is probably one of the reasons it is such a wonderful treat. I have eaten the vastly expensive kind which is flown in from California out of season, but I would not even recommend that.

Again, the French tend to produce thick, fat, pale asparagus, known as Argenteuil asparagus, which is not nearly so good as the fine English variety. But both the French and Italians produce a particularly slender, dark green asparagus which is very good and not unlike the wild variety which grows to my certain knowledge in south-west France, and no doubt in many other parts of Europe. When you see a Frenchman taking a walk you can be pretty sure that he has some ulterior motive – perhaps a mushroom, a snail – or a bunch of asparagus. Asparagus is usually served as a separate dish. It is too good to be wasted as a vegetable or mere side dish. Undoubtedly the English have the edge on the French when they serve their asparagus

hot with melted butter, rather than cold with vinaigrette, but there are some other greedy people – possibly Belgians – who have been known to serve their asparagus hot with melted butter and a soft boiled egg. You dip the asparagus first into the butter and then into the egg. A delicious idea indeed, and if you think of it from the point of view of the egg it makes a change from the usual soldiers or fingers of toast.

In fact asparagus and egg is a wonderful combination and, if you find that your garden does not produce enough asparagus to satisfy all your guests, you can make use of the little you have by putting the tips in scrambled eggs.

The best new potatoes – and usually the most expensive – come from Jersey. But they are worth the extra money. They have more taste and are easier to scrape than most other kinds. I have been bitterly disappointed in my time by French new potatoes. Considering their reputation as vegetable cooks, it is strange that the French should fall down over artichokes, asparagus and new potatoes. In France new potatoes are sold ready peeled in plastic packets. No self-respecting Englishman would touch them. Of course, if you live in the country

and have a greenhouse you can be digging your own new potatoes by May and can cock a snook at the Channel Islands and Spain.

As an alternative to mint and butter, cream and chopped tarragon can be added to new potatoes – either way they are irresistible.

The glory of fresh summer vegetables is that they are an adornment to any meal. With them about, there is no need for the anxious cook to fuss over rich sauces and complicated puddings.

May is a really wonderful month as not only do artichokes and asparagus appear on the scene, but it is the time of year when people begin to think of eating salmon. Several rather spoiled people of my acquaintance have recently complained to me that they have been having too much salmon. They never want to see another delicately poached pink fish resting in a bed of cucumber with a bowl of mayonnaise or *sauce verte* by its side. They don't even want a hot poached salmon borne to the table with a forthy, creamy white hollandaise sauce. Surfeiting, the appetite has sickened and so died. Poor them.

Never mind, we must be compassionate and rational in all things. This surfeit has no doubt been brought about by the fact that, with the introduction of farmed salmon on a large scale, salmon has become comparatively cheap and is therefore no longer quite such a rare treat.

In a minute the whole of France will also be sickened by the sight of salmon poached or otherwise, since every restaurant from the simplest to the very grandest now invariably includes it on the menu. Three star chefs from Reims to Les Baux are probably choosing their rosy fish at this very moment. At the famous Hôtel des Troisgros in Roanne "*escalope de saumon à l'oseille*" is even listed as a *spécialité de la maison*.

Not long ago I had the exquisite treat of lunching at Michel Guérard's sumptuous restaurant at Eugénie-les-Bains in south-western France. I did not choose salmon, but it was certainly on the menu.

In his beautiful book *La Grande Cuisine Minceur*, Michel Guérard gives a recipe for what he calls *hure de saumon au citron et poivre vert*. This is an elegant kind of salmon terrine which not only looks wonderful but tastes wonderful too and which might serve as an alternative dish for those poor souls who, like the poet Baudelaire, are desperately searching for something new. This terrine is made with alternative layers of flaked fish and a mixture of chopped hard-boiled eggs, diced lemon and peppers, whole green peppercorns, chopped

shallots, chervil and tarragon. The jellied stock must be poured over a layer of the garnish and allowed to set in the refrigerator before another layer of fish is placed on top of it.

Another excellent salmon recipe comes from *The Gentle Art of Cookery* which has recently been re-published in paperback by the Hogarth Press. Here, a pound of boiled flaked salmon is placed in a bowl and over it is poured a mixture made with ½ pt. milk, 2 egg yolks, ¾ oz. butter, a little sugar, 4 tablespoons vinegar, gelatine, a dessertspoonful of flour, salt, mustard and cayenne. To the flour, mustard powder, sugar and cayenne is added the melted butter, the beaten egg yolks and the milk. When this has been thickened in a double saucepan, the vinegar is added and the gelatine. The whole mixture should be placed in a mould, and served cold, with horse-radish sauce. Surprisingly enough the result is absolutely delicious.

Some people speak of using flaked salmon with cream, salt and pepper as a sauce for pasta. I have had this but am not sure quite how much I like it. The consistency of fish is not altogether satisfactory for pasta. In fact when one thinks of pasta and fish, *spaghetti alle vongole* inevitably comes to mind, and I think that the very presence of the clam shells makes the world of difference to the presentation. Besides which a delicate fish like salmon is, to my mind, wasted among all that pasta. But, there is no doubt that, where fish may not be ideal with pasta, it is ideal with rice, which brings us to the eternal argument about kedgeree. There are those who believe that it should always be made with haddock, and those who will only consider it when it is made with salmon. I stand somewhere between the two. One of my sisters-in-law makes the most delicious kedgeree with a mixture of smoked haddock and plain white fish and someone else I know has even been known to use kippers.

If you are using salmon in kedgeree you should certainly not mix it with another smoked fish, of that I am certain.

People sometimes fill rather nasty, greasy little vol-au-vent cases with salmon, but then vol-au-vent cases hide a multitude of sins. But flake your salmon and add it and a good helping to thick cream to a béchamel sauce, whip in an egg yolk and a little grated Gruyère. Put the filling into a ready-cooked pastry case and heat through in the oven, or fill pancakes with the same mixture.

A salmon soufflé too can be a glorious and a pretty thing. But perhaps most delicious of all are salmon fish-cakes. There is no need at all to add mashed potato to fish-cakes. Merely mix your flaked fish into a thick béchamel sauce to which you have added an egg yolk. Allow the mixture to cool before rolling the cakes in freshly ground white breadcrumbs. Cook the fish-cakes quickly in deep fat and serve with fried parsley. You will never want to eat another pre-packed fish-cake in your life.

But for my part, much as I appreciate all these things, I cannot imagine a day when my eyes won't light up and my mouth water at the sight of a traditional poached salmon with hollandaise sauce – for, as the old proverb says, 'fish must swim thrice – once in the water, a second time in the sauce, and a third time in the wine in the stomach.'

Nor would I be very pleased if my guests' faces fell as I brought my dish of salmon to the table. And, if I were to go so far as to serve it to a group of unknown guests gathered at my house before going on to some grand ball, I would expect them to clap their hands in glee.

In the olden days when I was young, May was the month in which people began to give dances, but times have changed and the children of yesterday's débutantes have, thank God for their sakes, flown away to the universities. So now most balls given for twenty-first birthdays or whatever tend to take place at the end of June or the beginning of July when the universities have closed their doors on the students and when the students have gone away to their well-earned three-months holiday.

But perhaps Mrs Thatcher's and Sir Keith Joseph's education cuts and their punitive treatment of students, combined with the massive scale of unemployment, will force people back on to the dance floors and the young will persuade their parents to throw great balls for them throughout the year so that they can grimace and gyrate mindlessly as the country finally sinks into the sea or disappears in a puff of smoke.

Perhaps they will also be able to persuade their parents that, however undiscriminating young people may be, they should not necessarily be treated as such, for how then will they ever learn to discriminate? I remember in my youth being mortally offended at the suggestion made by some that any old food would do for us – we couldn't tell good from bad anyway. Similarly I see faint expressions of horror cross my own children's faces if the same thing is hinted at in their presence.

I do not know whether it was as a result of this attitude or because people were so much less conscious of good food in those days but, when I first grew up, dinner before a dance consisted, as often as not, of chicken in white sauce served with either mashed or roast potatoes and carrots in white sauce. If it wasn't chicken in white sauce it would probably be chicken Maryland which, in my opinion, is quite one of the most disgusting dishes on earth. I have horrible memories of soggy bananas, tinned pineapple and greasy batter. There was never any gravy and the whole thing lay like a lump of lead on one's stomach.

Things must have improved since then although I sometimes wonder exactly to what extent. I recently served a *salade dite chaude* to a group of young persons before a dance. An Old Etonian squinted into the salad bowl and said: "I always like to look before I leap."

In any case, there is no real reason why food served before a dance should be any different to food at any other dinner party except that, as my daughter pointed out, you want to be able to dance.

So, although dinner before a summer dance may not need to be sparkling and romantic – with a hint of things to come but . . . it should at least be elegant.

Some of the most delicious soups are iced summer soups. Lettuce and lovage soup is one of the very best. The lettuce and a good two handfuls of lovage leaves should be melted in butter with an onion and seasoning and then put into a blender with some stock. Add a good quantity of milk and leave the soup in the fridge for several hours before serving it. Add a generous amount of thick cream at the last minute. This soup is quite excellent if made with lovage alone. Fresh peas can be made into a soup in the same way. So can ripe avocados which of course require no onions and no cooking. Avocado soup cannot be made too far ahead of time as it will go brown. It should, in any case, be covered up to prevent this from happening. Chopped chives should be sprinkled over the soup.

Try not to have chicken for your main course. Chicken is dull partly because it is cheap and therefore too often served, and partly because it rarely tastes of anything but fish in England. Roast duck is far better and more unusual. The trouble is, of course, that one duck only feeds four people but at this time of year duck is delicious served with nothing but fresh green peas.

If you cannot afford salmon, how about lamb? Do not serve roast potatoes for dinner, but tiny new ones. There is no need for another vegetable apart from a green salad – but baby carrots won't go amiss.

As I have said, I squeeze the juice of half an orange over a leg – or shoulder – of lamb before putting it in the oven. Add the rest of the orange juice to the gravy. Do not thicken your gravy, neither add wine to it. Vegetable water is much better – even the water from the new

potatoes. Some say do and some say don't stick a couple of cloves of garlic into the meat. I say do. I also put a twig of rosemary underneath it and on top of it.

What about the pudding? There is nothing better than profiteroles if you have the time. Unfortunately everyone loves them so it is hard to make enough. I think they are better filled with ice-cream than with anything else. Make sure that only the best chocolate – chocolate Menier – is used for the sauce. And remember the same chocolate should be used in a mousse.

The next best thing to profiteroles might be a strawberry tart. This can be made well in advance. It is economical on strawberries, beautiful to look at and utterly delicious.

If you wish to serve strawberries on their own, then why not, for a change, pour a little red wine or orange juice over them as they do in Italy? I hear cries of "shame" but I genuinely prefer them served like that, without cream.

A wonderful fruit salad can be made with halved strawberries, melon and split almonds. Then there are fools. Most people love a good raspberry or gooseberry fool which should be served with a variety of smart biscuits.

Just be careful not to start your dinner with pea soup and to end it with gooseberry fool. You might serve them the wrong way round.

May Wines

It is a terrible thing to advertise marital disagreements in this way, but my wife's habit of pouring new wine over strawberries, in what D.H. Lawrence called the Italian manner, has always appalled me. It spoils the strawberries, spoils the wine and prevents one drinking anything else. It is rather like mixing Guinness with cheap champagne (or, even worse, expensive champagne). I think and hope that the taste for Black Velvet, as the Guinness-champagne mixture was called, has died a natural death. It was particularly popular among undergraduates trying to cut a dash, who could not accept the cruelty of life that the rich can serve champagne and the poor can serve Guinness, but only bloody fools mix them together.

Fashionable folk nowadays, as I explained in April, decry the idea of serving sweet Bordeaux with strawberries or raspberries, saying that the sweetness of the fruit detracts from the sweetness of the wine and turns it into the sort of dry Semillon which the Australians make so well nowadays. They say that these wonderful, luscious wines from Sauternes should be drunk straight, as an apéritif, or possibly with fresh foie gras (which they insist, by another quirk of fashion, in covering with jammy sauces).

All this strikes me as nonsense. Sauternes drunk as an apéritif is altogether too overpowering: its enormous sugar level prepares one for nothing else. it is like eating a Mars Bar immediately before luncheon. However, a single glass of some lighter version, like Loupiac or Cérons, with cheese straws for accompaniment, is a reasonable preparation for luncheon in summer. Neither strawberries nor raspberries are very sweet in England, and raw sugar, whether granulated white or crystalline brown, adds as much grit as sweetness. It is only cooked sugar which is excessively sweet. My idea of heaven on earth remains strawberries or raspberries and cream with a Château d'Yquem of 1967, or perhaps 1976 at a pinch. Trumpets are an optional extra. But no honest Briton can nowadays afford Château d'Yquem except possibly the Duke of Westminster, so one must make do with one of the other châteaux which, in a good year, are very nearly as good and usually less than a quarter of the price: Rieussec, Coutet, Climens, Guiraud, Suduiraut, Filhot, Sigalas-Rabaud ... These wines can still be found in the bottom of the 'E' range if one buys them young enough. My own view about Sauternes is that it can perfectly well be drunk at six years old. There is a different taste of very old Sauternes which is also delicious, but which loses some of the fruitiness and is not, in my opinion, really worth waiting for. Those who cannot afford proper Sauternes might cross the river to Saint-Croix-du-Mont and Loupiac whose wines are indistinguishable in their best years, and much cheaper. The best I ever found was a Château Les Roques 1983 Loupiac which was costing only £3.15 in October 1985, putting it safely – and almost unbelievably for such a concentration of natural sweetness and fruit – in range 'C'.

Those who are frightened of being thought unfashionable or unadventurous might try one of the famous sweet 'n' sour wines from the Loire Valley: Bonnezeaux, Quarts de Chaume or Coteaux de Layon. These are made from the chenin blanc grape which also gives us much of the foul rubbish from Vouvray and Anjou, but Bonnezeaux (pronounced exactly like the dog's name) in particular is highly concentrated both in the sweetness of its approach and in the sharp nip at the end. Bonnezeaux is quite easy to find in the 'C' range when young, though it mounts to 'D' and even 'E' with a little age. But these wines are worth trying. Some people think them the perfection of a dessert wine, claiming that the long, sweet finish of a Barsac or Sauternes always turns to dust and ashes in the end, leaving the drinker with a hot mouth and throat and general feeling of over-indulgence. Personally, I do not mind if I never drink another Bonnezeaux, but everybody should try it once.

So much for strawberries and raspberries. Globe artichokes, like asparagus, ruin any wine they come into contact with. The reason for this, which is bio-chemical, was explained to me by an immensely boring German I sat next to at lunch one day. He also told me why asparagus makes urine smell, but I refused to listen. The sad fact remains that the only thing to drink with either of these delicious vegetables is water. In the case of artichokes, the biochemical whatnot can hang around in the mouth, and it is a good idea to eat something else before drinking wine.

The same might be said of *profiteroles au chocolat* and chocolate mousse, although I have heard various quack solutions put forward for the dreadful problem of having nothing to drink with chocolate. Perhaps a really strong *muscat*, whether from Beaumes de Venise or further south, or Fonseca's delicate moscatel might conquer a chocolate mousse, but cooked sugar should be kept well away from the great dessert wines of Bordeaux, and chocolate kills them.

Salmon is such a delicate fish that I hesitate to be didactic. Where it is served with mayonnaise, which drowns its taste in any case, I would recommend a really beefy white Burgundy, or even better a buttery Californian Chardonnay. The same advice would apply to hot salmon in any buttery sauce, like hollandaise, but where butter gives way to cream I would try something lighter – Paul Masson has a beautiful Chardonnay in the 'C'/'D' range, while Mondavi's ordinary Chardonnay (as opposed to his Reserve) is still be be found in 'E'. The Australians produce some excellent light Chardonnays as well as their heavier ones – Rosemount, Brown Bros. and Penfold are my favourites, all to be found in 'D'. Finally, there are the excellent and ever improving white wines from the Mâconnais, all safely in 'D', but I would not drink a sauvignon-based white with salmon on the grounds that it nearly always overwhelms it. This rules out Sancerre, Pouilly Fumé, most of Bergerac and Graves, although occasionally you find small growers concentrating on a dry semillon, which goes excellently well with salmon in any form. This should be at the very bottom of 'D', but Australians traditionally produce even better dry semillons which can often be found in 'C'.

Otherwise May is a month of optimism and hope when one might feel inclined to experiment with new wines, new regions. Among whites, I would point people's noses towards the Côtes de Gascogne, where there are some excellent new whites being made from such improbable grapes as Colombard and Folle Blanche (otherwise known as Gros Plant). They are crisp and aromatic, without being sour or thin, and cost nothing – in the bottom range of 'B'. Most Vinho Verde reaching these shores from Portugal still strikes me as being sugared and really quite nasty. For red wines in May I should look to the Touraine – some of their Gamays are now serious rivals to Beaujolais, and at half the price. An elegant variation is to serve Sancerre Rouge made from the pinot noir grape although you would never guess it. The best ones – Vacheron's Clos des Romains is an example – smell of raw meat and taste of malt. It is not a very serious wine and not at all cheap, being high 'D', but it makes a change.

JUNE

One of the pleasantest things about the summer is to be able – occasionally at least – to eat out of doors. But it is extremely important to see that meals eaten outside are done so in comfort. The sun, more than anything else, makes eating out of doors uncomfortable. It is essential to eat in the shade unless you like tepid wine, melting butter, greasy salad and greasy cheese.

I remember returning from school to eat beautifully cut cucumber sandwiches in the shade of the huge beech trees which grew on the lawns of my childhood home. Never since have I enjoyed a cucumber sandwich so much. I would suggest then that where you eat outside is just as important as what you eat.

If you have a shortage of beech trees, almost any other tree will do – or indeed a shady corner of a terrace. Of course if you are planning to eat out of doors in the evening – and it is rarely warm enough for that in England – there is no need to worry about shade.

Apart from hot sunshine, one of the great disadvantages of eating out of doors is that it involves so much fetching and carrying. Try to find a spot then which is shady, near to your kitchen door or window and where you can conveniently leave a table outside. (I am not of course referring to barbecues or straightforward picnics here.) If you plan to make a habit of eating in the same spot, a few tubs of geraniums may add to your pleasure.

I was brought up to believe that you only eat soup for lunch North of the Border, so for the purposes of this argument let us suppose that you are either North of the Border or that you are eating your dinner outside. What could be nicer on a fine summer's evening than iced soup to begin with?

An excellent iced soup can be made by melting an onion and a finely chopped, peeled cucumber in butter with a little mint and then blending the vegetables with some good chicken stock. I prefer cucumber soup made without the addition of cream and so proper stock should be used here rather than a cube. Broad beans (podded and peeled), spinach and sorrel can all be made into delicious cold soups. And of course everyone has their own particular version of gazpacho.

But what about the main course which should not involve too much fetching and carrying? Presumably you will have sensibly laid your meat plates under your soup plates as the French do. It is surprising how rarely people do this in England.

After your soup you could serve cold cutlets and mint sauce and a salad. It is odd how rarely one comes across home-made mint sauce these days. I cannot think why since mint is easy to come by and the sauce takes all of five minutes. Chop the mint finely with the sugar, add boiling water and leave to infuse and cool about an hour before adding the vinegar. In my opinion bought mint jelly is no substitute for the real thing.

You may, as you read this, be dreaming of salmon trout and mayonnaise, or even of cold chicken and mayonnaise, but to my mind mayonnaise is absolutely not at its best in the sunshine. Neither is Camembert, nor is Brie or any other full fat cheese. In any case Camemberts tend to be better during the winter months. English cheeses also have a tendency to sweat. I would recommend a handsome piece of Gruyère or Emmenthal. Emmenthal can be delicious although it is too often cut up and wrapped in horrid pieces of plastic.

After such a simple meal you may welcome a glorious pudding like a strawberry mousse made as you would make a strawberry fool with strawberries, icing sugar, whipped cream, a drop of lemon juice and with the addition of the whipped whites of eggs. The mousse should be left in the refrigerator for several hours before it is served. Or if the weather is nice enough you may have made a strawberry ice cream, or a strawberry water-ice. I have no especial weakness for water-ices but somehow prefer them – for reasons of taste as well as appearance – if two flavours are served together, like blackcurrant and strawberry or strawberry and raspberry. These fruit sorbets are delicious with a drop of alcohol like *eau de vie de prune* or *framboise* poured over them.

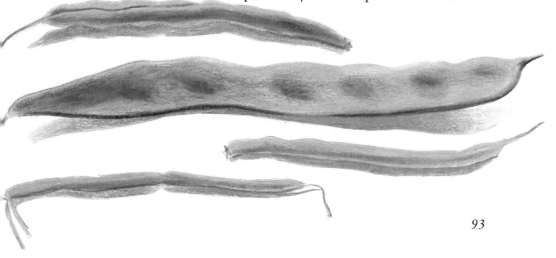

One of the most delicious summer recipes I know is Elizabeth David's recipe for *oeufs mollets à la creme aux fines herbes*. The inconvenience of these from the point of view of eating outside is that they need to be cooked for two or three minutes just before they are served. But if you are eating near your kitchen it would be quite possible to have them as a first course, or even as a main course for a light luncheon. Nothing is more mouth-watering nor more delicate than these peeled, soft-boiled eggs lightly heated in fresh cream with pepper, a handful of chopped herbs and a touch of garlic.

I discovered in France an unusual way of eating Spanish omelettes. Make two omelettes with plenty of chopped onion and potato, leave them to cool. When they are cold spread one of them with thick, home-made tomato sauce. Press the second omelette down on top of the sauce. Cut your omelettes like a cake and serve them with a green salad and you will have an excellent simple lunch or supper and one which would be pleasant to eat out of doors provided the midges don't bite your legs nor the wasps creep into your wine.

If, like me, you are lucky enough to live in the country and to have a large greenhouse, the very word "salad" takes on a new meaning. You can, even after the coldest spring, pick great lettuces like royal hats in early May. By July, you are enjoying your first tomatoes and gathering vast bunches of basil daily.

Living in the country has, of course, its disadvantages. Our West Country shops are not filled throughout the winter months with beautiful red-leaved cripplingly expensive radicchio, nor can we easily buy strawberries out of season. Cabbages and carrots are our winter fare.

But come the salad days . . . how happy we are then. And by June the salad days should be here to stay for a while at least and salads are bound to play a large part in your life if the weather is nice enough for you to be eating out of doors.

One of the first points to consider, where salad is concerned, is how to make the dressing. Whether or not to put sugar in your vinaigrette, whether to use mustard, which type of oil to use, and so forth. I have heard bitter arguments waged on all these points – arguments fit to divide families – and I, like most other people, feel strongly about them all.

When I make salad dressings, I usually use a little Dijon mustard, white or red wine vinegar, sometimes cider vinegar, usually Greek olive oil or sunflower seed oil if I don't want a strong taste.

I absolutely never put sugar in salad dressing as it then reminds me of something rather nasty with milk in it which is served in Germany with *salat*. But I must admit that I do occasionally sprinkle a tiny amount of sugar over grated carrots or tomatoes to bring out their naturally sweet taste.

A friend of mine brings back from Spain the most delicious one-hundred-year-old sherry vinegar. There is nothing to touch it, but alas it is unobtainable in this country although you may be able to get a good ordinary sherry vinegar.

Perhaps the best vinegar is one which you have made yourself. Put an inch of wine vinegar in the bottom of a wine bottle and gradually fill the bottle with remains of wine. Leave the cork out of the bottle and cover the top with muslin to prevent flies getting in. By the end of six months you will have some excellent vinegar. The better the wine you have used, the better your vinegar will be. People sometimes forget that the quality of their vinegar is quite as important as the quality of their oil.

Some of my French friends make a particularly good salad dressing with a good dessertspoonful of Dijon mustard into which they gradually mix olive oil, beating hard as they do so, until the dressing has reached the consistency of mayonnaise.

Of course the dressing which you decide to make may depend as much on your mood as on the salad. Personally, as I eschew sugar, so would I always eschew anything American called Rokefort (sic). But a sauce rémoulade may make a welcome change. For a rémoulade carefully blend the oil and vinegar as for a mayonnaise into the crushed yolks of three eggs.

"*Moi je dis toujours qu'un repas sans salade ce n'est pas un repas,*" says a middle-class lady about to turn the salad in a huge bowl in Bunuel's film *Le discret charme de la bourgeoisie*. It is difficult not to agree with this lady who, poor thing, as a result of some appalling disaster was eventually deprived of her salad. And luckily there is no limit to the different salads one can serve – especially in summer.

And of course different occasions deserve different salads although a plain green salad is almost always suitable. A good green salad can be enhanced with a few chopped lovage leaves, with some chervil, some tarragon or some basil. The chopped white of an egg is also an agreable addition to a lettuce salad. A green salad is particularly good if you turn it about half an hour before you serve it and then add the ground black pepper which sticks to the wet lettuce leaves.

Most people like avocado pears, but they are available in winter and have, to my mind, been rather over-done in recent years, so I wouldn't really choose an avocado pear if I wanted to make a rather better than usual salad. Instead, if you can find it, add a few leaves of roquette, a dark dandelion-shaped, bitter leaf which is common in France and Italy. Or add some cold French beans or a thinly sliced courgette.

I think it is true to say that green salads or "mixed" salads are far better in Italy than anywhere else. I certainly remember being amazed at the age of about sixteen when I first went to Italy by the glorious mixtures of lettuce, fennel, roquette or *ruchetta* and finely, finely sliced radishes.

Another Italian favourite which it is always a pleasure to see displayed in most good trattorias is an *insalata di mare*.

For an *insalata di mare* your dressing should be made with oil and lemon rather than vinegar and ideally you should use a mixture of *calamari* (squid or inkfish), shrimps and mussels. If you have no *calamari* you can use scallops, crab or indeed any firm white fish flaked.

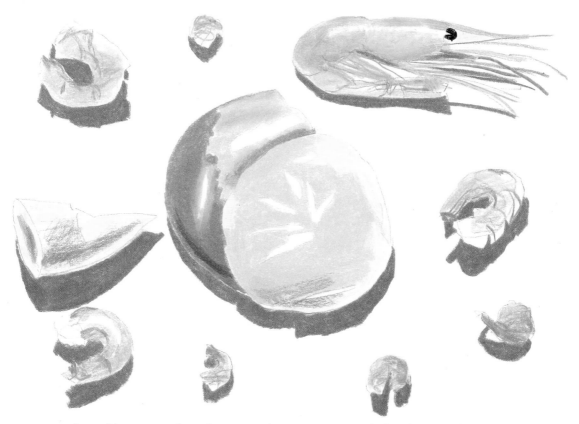

If you like an *insalata di mare*, why not a meat salad? The French often serve the remains of their boiled beef from a *pot au feu* diced and dressed with a vinaigrette to which they have added a crushed hard-boiled egg and a handful of chopped mixed herbs. Accompanied by a lightly dressed green salad this makes a delicious summer meal. Cold tongue can be dressed in the same way.

Another thing which I have found the French doing more and more often in recent years is making salad with macaroni or other types of pasta. Sometimes it can be good but I am not entirely sure how much I really like it as it tends to have a sort of "left-over" look about it even if the pasta has been especially cooked for the salad. A good way of making pasta salad, though, is to mix the cold pasta with some diced ham and to mix in some mayonnaise.

One of the strangest salads in the world is Russian salad which as far as I can remember used to turn up with monotonous regularity at school and at dreadful teenage dances. There is no doubt about it that Russian salad is a thoroughly nasty thing, and neither is its taste in any way enhanced by its appearance since it looks like nothing so much as sick. I have never yet met anyone who admitted to liking Russian salad or who disagreed with my view of it and yet it still puts in an occasional appearance. Occasional, cries my daughter: all the bloody time – in pubs, cafeterias, aeroplanes and still apparently, to this day, in schools. What mysterious and malevolent forces combine, I wonder, to perpetuate the life of this apparently universally loathed concoction?

Just as Russian salad is universally loathed, so potato salad is universally loved and I have a sister-in-law who makes a particularly good one. Pour the vinaigrette into which you have grated an onion over the potatoes while they are still hot and when they are cold stir in a little mayonnaise or sauce rémoulade.

There are various things which you can do with a potato salad. You can for instance add some chopped anchovies and a chopped hard-boiled egg or a few capers. I don't especially like capers but think that used occasionally and sparingly they can be good. Another excellent way of making potato salad is to mix the cooked sliced potatoes with some diced, firm eating apples and dress with mayonnaise.

Whereas potato salad is always served as an accompaniment to something else, rice salads are a meal in themselves. I had a dreadful craze for making rice salads a few years ago, but the doctrine of the thirty-seventh oyster eventually applied and I found that I had had one too many with the result that I hardly ever make them now; but one should do really, as most people enjoy them occasionally, besides which they are easy to make for large numbers. Always, as with potatoes, add the vinaigrette to the rice while it is still warm. To the cooked rice add chopped tomatoes, tunny fish, garlic, peas, spring onions and black olives.

Some people add diced cheese to rice salads. I think this is a dreadful mistake and one which I would avoid at all costs although a surprisingly good addition comes in the shape of lentils.

This does not mean that I never like cheese in salad. The Italians make a delicious salad from a mixture of green beans, tomatoes, black olives, lettuce, fennel and slices of fetta cheese.

Red peppers also need to be used with discretion. I hate to see lumps of them or of green peppers, cropping up all over the place. They have such a definite taste and consistency that I feel they should play a leading part or no part at all. They are, for instance, delicious when they are stuffed or in a salad of their own when they have been grilled until the skins are blackened. The skins are then scraped off, the peppers are cut into strips and dressed with oil and possibly a little garlic.

Naturally in summer time there is an infinite variety of vegetables which are available for salad; for instance broad beans are almost better in a salad than they are hot, so long as the outer skin has been removed and they are mixed with a handful of chopped parsley. And artichokes, provided they are small, can be trimmed, sliced and eaten raw with a little good coarse salt.

Then there is the old favourite *salade niçoise* with lettuce, garlic, anchovies, hard-boiled eggs, black olives and tomatoes.

With regard to tomatoes, it may well be true to say that one swallow does not make a summer, but a few home-grown tomatoes certainly do. I am sure that I make more tomato salads throughout the summer than I do any other kind of salad. And I never tire of it especially if I have some fresh basil to add to it.

If you are making a tomato salad, pour boiling water over the tomatoes so as to remove their skins, slice them, lay them in a flat dish, season them, sprinkle them with chopped chives or basil and add a little olive oil. No other dressing is necessary. The French use under-ripe tomatoes for salad and the riper ones for stuffing.

The more one thinks about salads, the more different, delicious things leap to mind and it is easy to imagine sitting endlessly out of doors on long, warm June evenings playing with a *salade aux épinards cuits* or toying with a mixture of prawns and mushrooms – there are indeed a thousand different wonderful salads so that there should never ever be any need to eat a quartered tomato, a bottled beetroot and a lettuce leaf smothered in salad cream.

Instead, try making a *taboulé*. For six people you need $\frac{1}{2}$ lb. of raw couscous, 1 lb. of tomatoes, 6 ozs. finely chopped onion, 6 tablespoon-fuls of olive oil, the juice of three lemons, a handful of chopped parsley and a handful of chopped mint, salt and pepper. Put the couscous and chopped tomatoes with their juice in the salad bowl. Add the onions and herbs, seasoning, oil and lemon juice. Mix the salad and leave it in a cool place for two or three hours, stirring it from time to time to ensure that the couscous "cooks" in the juices.

June Wines

June is not a month for serious wines of any colour except white, and no serious wine should ever be drunk out of doors. One enjoys really quite indifferent wine with good food in warm weather, which may explain why so many people come back from their holidays raving about some particular wine they have "discovered" in Provence or Sicily, Sardinia or even Corsica. When, after some difficulty, they find where to buy it in England, or even import it themselves with even greater trouble, and drink it themselves at twice the price in a heated English dining room with the rain pattering on the windows, it is almost always a disappointment. This gives rise to the myth of wine which can't travel. Nowadays, when nearly all wine is imported in bottles, there should be no such thing as a wine which cannot travel – unless it happens to freeze or boil in transit. This is a real risk now that containers are stored on deck – they *have* been known to freeze on the run from Bordeaux and Oporto, although I have not yet experienced any boiled wine from Australia, where the temperature on deck, crossing the equator, should be deleterious. Nothing on earth will stop English fools from putting their claret close to the fire in order to warm it up when they have been too lazy to bring it from the cellar in time. This *always* ruins the wine, stirring up the acids and evaporating the alcohol. Others pour boiling water over the bottle, which seems to have an even worse effect. Perhaps there will be a ready market for Australian boiled wine among such people, since that is how they expect wine to taste.

But the real reason for the myth of wine which cannot travel is that traditionally the English have drunk much better wine in England than they do abroad, as a result of the flat-rate Excise Duty on wine whereby one paid exactly the same exorbitant duty on a bottle of plonk as one did on a bottle of Lafite. With the arrival of 15 per cent VAT on top, and with the catastrophic jump in the prices of the best-known French wines, all this is changing, but the British wine trade still shops around very seriously indeed for its cheaper wines and the standard of wine sold here is very high. That little-known rosé from the hills above St Tropez which tasted absolutely delicious with moules marinière under the multi-coloured parasol in the old port is still recognized for what it is when drunk in England – a second-rate local wine in a silly bottle.

It took me a long time to recogonize this simple truth. Every year I take my family to eat a bouillabaisse near the Mediterranean town of Leucate. Every year we drink the same wine with it – a Listel Gris de Gris from the sandy vineyards of the Golfe de Lyon. Every year we remark how particularly delicious it is. Eventually I tracked it down to Les Amis du Vin, in Shepherds Bush, who were selling it in the lower

'B' range. Carried triumphantly back to Somerset, correctly chilled and served with an excellent fish soup at a dinner party in November, it revealed itself as absolute rubbish. But we still drink it every year in Leucate with cries of delight.

"It is easy to imagine sitting endlessly out of doors on long, warm June evenings playing with a *salade aux épinards cuits* or toying with a mixture of prawns and mushrooms," writes my wife, meditating about the month of June. One could even imagine eating jellied eels in a jacuzzi at the North Pole on Midsummer's Day, which lasts all of

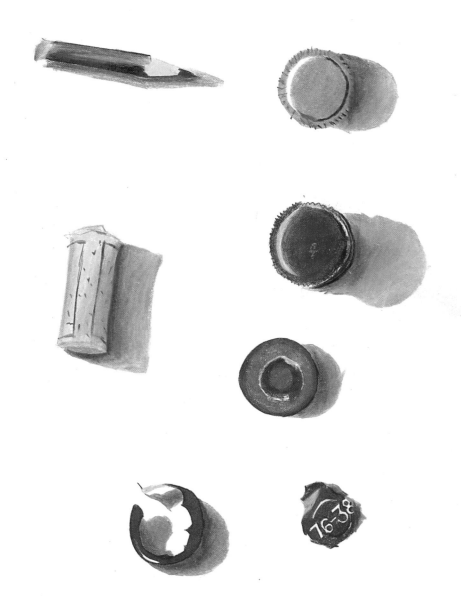

three weeks in those parts. Aquavit would be the thing to drink, or possibly one of the flavoured vodkas. In reality, I do not suppose that many English folk eat out of doors in June more than once or twice a year, even on picnics. If the weather is warm, the setting agreeable and the food good enough – I was slightly alarmed by her emphasis on salads, which may be perfectly all right in their place, but scarcely constitute what you or I would call a meal – then almost any wine will taste good.

This is the great moment to experiment. Every wine warehouse, cash and carry or chain store has rows and rows of cheap wine. Avoid the obvious disaster areas – anything called "moelleux", *anything* from Anjou, any Euro-blend in a German-style bottle, anything called Hirondelle – and buy a selection of half a dozen different cheapies. Some will be foul, but others will be all right and at least one will probably be hailed as a Major Discovery. The problem with buying cheap wines at random when you are not entertaining is that you feel bound to finish them, or waste the money. This is where guests come in useful. You announce your out of doors luncheon or dinner party as a Grand Tasting occasion, which is a Fun Idea. You offer half a dozen or more different bottles of wine, depending upon the number of guests, and make sure they all have a glass of each, thereby finishing the bottles. You listen politely to their inarticulate, mumbled comments on each or you might even ask them to write them down, as if eating and drinking were some kind of paper game. When the guests have gone you throw away their bits of paper and try to forget all the idiotic, inappropriate comments they have made. But you should have a reasonable idea which of these cheap wines is worth buying again. That is the only way I know of choosing cheap wines which does not involve great suffering and unnecessary expense. It is no good listening to the advice of experts, or personal recommendations from friends, because these cheap wines on the shelves are always changing – or at any rate changing labels – and by the time the news of a good cheapie has reached you it will almost certainly have disappeared.

Having identified a good cheapie, one should buy as much as one can afford, up to a month's supply or the entire stock. This is also the best way of choosing a cheap wine for a young persons' party or, indeed, any party where one is not concerned to cut a dash. In my own case, I have the advantage of being asked to most trade tastings so I do not have to make my guests jump through hoops in this way. But these tastings are quite disagreeable occasions, involving as many as sixty wines at a time, and I would not wish them on anybody who was not involved in the wine trade.

June, as I say, is not a time of year for drinking serious wines, except on the rare occasions when a serious meal is being served – indoors or out of doors – to a seriously discriminating guest, when one might bring out an excellent white Burgundy, white Bordeaux, Californian Chardonnay or Sauvignon from the Loire, not to mention my own favourite, the absurdly over-priced but exquisite Condrieu, made in the northern Rhône from the disappearing Viognier grape. But I shall be treating of serious white wines in July and August. Where you have a June guest eating out of doors, who is a good friend and sound judge of wine, I generally produce some of the oddities I have discovered in the year, red wines which strike me as very good but which one would hesitate to serve on a formal occasion: an interesting Chilean Cabernet Sauvignon called Viña Linderos priced in 'B' or low 'C', made from ungrafted pre-phylloxera vines; an exceptionally fruity Zinfandel from California – Wente Bros make the cheapest good one I have yet discovered; a beautifully thick Cabernet-Malbec from Stanley Leasingham, in Clare Valley, Australia; one of Robin Yapp's discoveries among the experimental wine-makers of Provence, often now growing the classic grapes of Cabernet, Merlot and Syrah. The only danger, as I say, is that people's enthusiasm for wines drunk in these circumstances may out-run their ordinary caution, and they will find themselves going out to buy cases and cases of wine which will look very odd when served at a dinner party in the winter – almost as if they are short-changing their guests. But that is their problem, not yours.

JULY

July is the time of year when tomatoes are plentiful and cheap and when, if you grow your own under glass, you will begin to be able to pick baskets each day.

In times gone by country housewives used to spend hours packing tomatoes into Kilner jars to store them for the winter. I grow a lot of tomatoes many of which I put straight into plastic bags and freeze. When they have been frozen they can be skinned under the hot tap in no time, unlike fresh ones which have to be plunged into boiling water, but, when frozen, they can only be used for sauce or soup or perhaps to thicken a stew like an ox-tail. Personally I never buy tomatoes in the winter months as they are not only expensive but perfectly tasteless and the tinned Italian ones are far better for sauces anyway.

Everyone has their own way of making tomato soup but one day, when I was feeling exhausted and was confronted by hoards of hungry people, I discovered the simplest and possibly the best way of making it. This recipe cannot be made with tinned tomatoes, however good they may be, but can be made with skinned frozen or fresh ones. Melt some butter in a pan with a chopped onion and a chopped clove of garlic. Add more than a pinch of preferably fresh thyme. If the herbs are melted in the butter at this stage, they taste stronger. If the tomatoes are fresh, chop them; frozen ones will easily dissolve into a pulp. Put the tomatoes in the pan and season with salt and decent amount of black pepper. I would use one tomato per person and a few extra. When the tomatoes are reduced to a pulp, add some water and a chicken stock cube. A tablespoon of tomato purée will also help. Leave the soup stewing for quite a long time – say an hour – but keep looking at it and, if necessary, add more water. The soup is them ready to serve. Some people may feel that this soup should be sieved, but I prefer it as it is, so long as it is sufficiently liquid. If it is stewed long enough it will not taste watery.

But in July the frozen tomato is momentarily a thing of the past and fresh tomatoes come into their own with a vengeance. I could happily eat tomato salad every day – in fact I almost do in the summer months and I agree with the French that the under-ripe ones are best for salad. Some French people put them in salad when they are still quite green.

One of the very best ways of eating tomatoes in salad is to slice them and lay them in a dish with some sliced Mozzarella cheese. Add salt, black pepper, good olive oil, chopped basil and, if you like, some chopped anchovies and some black olives. A few years ago I had occasion to spend a month alone in Florence and I used to eat this for lunch in a bar every day. If I could easily find good Mozzarella at home, I think I might eat it every day for the rest of my life.

Some people in Italy annoyingly tell you that you should never eat Mozzarella north of Naples and no doubt the best Mozzarella in the world comes from Naples – it certainly doesn't come from Denmark – but unfortunately we cannot always go to Naples for our Mozzarella so some of us are bound to make do with second best, and it is possible to buy good Mozzarella in the Italian shops in Soho and elsewhere. The best Mozzarella and of course the only true Mozzarella is made from buffalo milk – and it is occasionally possible to find even that.

Tomatoes baked in the oven for about twenty minutes with a little crushed garlic, salt, pepper, breadcrumbs and a knob of butter on top are so good and not often made except in French provincial restaurants where they nearly always come with your *biftek* and *frites*.

There are a thousand different ways of stuffing tomatoes – almost all of which are excellent. Raw ones can be stuffed with cold flaked haddock in mayonnaise, with crab or the tunny fish, with the remains of a rice sald, with chopped hard-boiled egg, onion and anchovies or with cold chicken and mayonnaise. Or they can be filled with a meat stuffing, baked and served hot.

I remember when I was a child my father suddenly had a bright idea about yellow tomatoes. Yellow tomatoes which were apparently the ones originally imported into Europe, were what we wanted and for several years we had them. It seems to me that as roses should not be blue so tomatoes should not be yellow. What on earth is wrong with the red ones we are used to? As far as I can remember the yellow ones did not taste any better than the red ones and they were certainly not so pretty. But they are still about and can occasionally be found lurking in strange places.

The wife of the French castrator, whom I have already mentioned in connection with lamb, used, when she had a glut of tomatoes, to make a tomato stew in a deep frying pan and into it she would break some eggs and allow them to poach gently. This is rather a messy, but delicious dish and should be served with good fresh bread. Or the tomatoes can be sliced, laid in a buttered fire-proof dish and baked. The eggs are broken into the dish when the tomatoes are nearly cooked, some cream is poured over the eggs and the dish is returned to the oven until the eggs are cooked.

An unusual and excellent way to eat tomatoes – and one which guests will welcome – is *à la crème*. Cook the halved tomatoes slowly in butter on both sides before pouring over some fresh cream. Mix the cream into the tomato juices but try to leave the tomato halves whole. Serve with a sprinkling of chopped fresh tarragon. When cooking halved tomatoes in a pan, the cut side should always be cooked first to avoid a total mess.

If you have a great many ripe tomatoes, skin them, chop them and melt them in a little olive oil – do not let them cook – season them and add masses of chopped, fresh basil. This makes a wonderfully fresh spaghetti sauce.

It is surpising how often a real tomato sauce can be disappointing. I am sure that one of the reasons for this is that people tend to cook it far too short a time.

For your tomato sauce, melt a chopped onion, a chopped carrot and some garlic in oil with a little fresh thyme. Add the peeled chopped tomatoes, salt and pepper and, if you want a strong sauce, a little concentrated tomato purée. Cook very slowly for three quarters of an hour. I don't usually sieve my tomato sauce but many people feel that it is better sieved.

In fact the best way to eat tomatoes, like grapes, is straight from the plant while they are still warm from the sun.

Although it is true to say that tomatoes are often over-used and baldly slapped on any old plate under the peculiarly unpleasant heading of garnish, they do have an important part to play in various minor ways. For instance they help to thicken a stew, they are excellent melted into a little butter with some garlic and mixed like this into your French beans, and of course they are wonderful with aubergines.

Fry separately in oil some sliced tomatoes and some sliced aubergines with a little garlic. Place the vegetables in alternate layers in a buttered dish and sprinkle with breadcrumbs. Add a few dots of butter or a little oil and brown in the oven.

As the summer progresses delicious fruits as well as tomatoes begin to capture the imagination and we no longer have to make do with those we grow ourselves since nowadays French and Spanish peaches, nectarines and melons reach our shops with amazing speed.

There is nothing more dreary than a bad fruit salad in which horrible pieces of soggy banana float around with oranges and apples and tinned mandarins or tangerines or clementines. The worst experience I have ever had with tinned tangerines was to have them served with artificial cream as an *hor d'oeuvre*. There may still be three very old ladies in South Kensington who think that this is an acceptable way to start a meal, but I rather doubt that there is anyone else.

I have tried to discover a name for a small instrument which I have with a wooden handle and a little bowl-shaped end. But to no avail. It never seems to appear in any list of required *batterie de cuisine* and it is even hard to find in the *Larousse Gastronomique* with all its fancy information. I finally tracked it down under *pommes de terre parisienne* for which potatoes I knew my instrument was necessary. There I was referred to *pommes noisette* where I discovered that my instrument comes in various sizes but still I could find no name. The best the *Larousse* could do was "round vegetable scooping spoon". I wonder how you say that in French. Since NATO becomes OTAN and AIDS becomes DISA, it must be something along the lines of spoon scooping vegetable round or perhaps its name is Rumpelstiltskin.

In any case with your "round vegetable scooping spoon" you can make a wonderful fruit salad by scooping out some small balls of melon and mixing them with some sliced preserved ginger. Melons also go well with strawberries and to these you can add a handful of split, blanched almonds. The almonds should be added at the last moment to prevent them from going soft. A further sophistication where melons are concerned is to mix the different coloured flesh of

different kinds of melons – the green Israeli variety with a honeydew melon and an orange Cavaillon – always remembering to use your "round vegetable scooping spoon". Finely chopped mint is delicious with melon as indeed it is with strawberries too.

Mint can also be used with a mixture of oranges and grapefruit. For this you need quite a lot of mint, equal quantities of the two fruits and a little sugar. This makes one of the prettiest and most refreshing fruit salads I know.

Another simple and excellent fruit dish is a compote of peaches. Choose ripe peaches and boil them in sugared water for about five or six minutes. When you have done this you will be able to skin the fruit easily. Arrange the peaches in a dish and pour a little of the syrup in which they have cooked over them. Serve them chilled and, if you feel like it, with a sauce made from pulped raspberries and, if possible, redcurrants and sugar. Frozen raspberries can perfectly well be used. A drop of lemon juice in the sauce will not go amiss. If you are feeling rich a dash of champagne will make a triumph of it.

If you live in the country, you may decide to treat your guests to elderflowers or acacia flowers fried in batter. This dish is exquisitely pretty and subtly delicious. Pick one or two heads per person of, say, elder, dip them into a thin batter, deep fry for them an instant and dip them into sugar as soon as you have removed them from the fat. The flowers will appear crystallised and elegant, their only disadvantage being that they should be eaten immediately. There is no need to expect your guests to eat the stalks. A squeeze of lemon juice will add to the flavour.

Recently, in Italy, I had an excellent pudding made from Ricotta cheese and sponge. I had never had it before and was delighted by it. For the sponge, you can use sponge fingers. Soak the biscuits in Maraschino and line a mould with them. If you don't like Maraschino there is no reason why you should not use Kirsch or even rum. The liqueur should be diluted with a little water first or you will find yourself using far too much. Put the Ricotta cheese through a sieve and beat it hard with sugar. Mix in a generous handful of candied peel and fill the mould with the cheese. Cover the cheese with more sponge fingers. Keep the pudding in the refrigerator until it is time to turn it out and serve it. Ricotta cheese is easily found in Italian shops.

But to my mind the finest, and most beautiful, pudding with which to herald the summer is a strawberry tart. The pre-cooked pastry base should be covered with a layer of *crème patissière* and the halved strawberries arranged carefully on top of this. For the glaze, use a pot of blackcurrant jelly. Melt the jelly with a little water and pour it very carefully over the fruit, leave it to set and wait for the cries of greedy delight from your guests. Even those ridiculous people who "make it a rule" never to eat puddings may be tempted. What an extraordinary rule that is anyway! It is not as if puddings are made to suffer like geese. Besides I was brought up to believe that one should eat what was put in front of one.

Queen of Puddings is perhaps the most unjustly usurped of all titles. The pudding which bears that name and which many of us were made to eat as children, like Russian salad, reminds me of sick. It may be rather childish to keep making this comparison but if there is anything in the world which has no right to resemble sick then it must be food. And no one can reasonably be expected to eat anything which has this unfortunate quality. All the same I must admit that I have discovered that people are not entirely with me on Queen of Pudding as they appear to be on Russian salad.

The real Queen of Puddings is a title with which I would crown a summer pudding.

Summer pudding must not be made with ready sliced bread which does not properly absorb the juice and I think it is best made with a mixture of raspberries, red-currants and blackcurrants, all of which should be plentiful in July. Some people use rhubarb, gooseberries and even strawberries. I hate cooked strawberries except in strawberry jam.

Stew your fruit in water with sugar added. Line your pudding basin with slices of white bread from which you have removed the crust and fill with the fruit and some of the juice. Keep the remainder of the juice aside. Cover the fruit with more slices of white bread and put the basin in the refrigerator with a plate and a weight on top of it. Leave the pudding in the refrigerator for several hours. Serve it turned out on a round dish with the remainder of the juice poured over it and accompanied by a lot of good thick cream.

If you are entertaining any French people in the summer I highly recommend giving them this pudding. They tend to be delighted by it.

Although the French appear to have no name for round vegetable scooping spoons, they do have one, however inadequate, for gooseberries which they call *groseilles à maquereau*. As the name seems to denote, these fruit are only used in France, to the best of my knowledge, in conjunction with mackerel – a dish which I for one have never ever eaten in France. Neither have I ever seen a gooseberry in France, but I have noticed that when my French friends come to England they are as delighted by gooseberries as they are by summer pudding and by rhubarb. Perhaps they are just delighted by the novelty as it has often occurred to me that the reason why the French have no rhubarb and no gooseberries is because neither rhubarb nor gooseberries are really very nice. The nearest I have come to rhubarb in France was when I saw it on a menu as an accompaniment to duck. If apples and oranges go with duck, I can see no very good reason why rhubarb should not but I remember feeling at the time that the chef was just trying to be clever.

I quite like rhubarb jam and I am pleased to see the rhubarb as it appears each year but I wish that it didn't set your teeth on edge. Gooseberries of course do the same thing but there's no harm in the occasional gooseberry fool, and gooseberry jam is delicious particularly if made with the addition of some elderflowers.

Both rhubarb jam and gooseberry jam can be used in a bastardisation of *fromage* Bar-le-duc. Red-currant jams traditionally come from Bar-le-duc, a town in the Meuse which is not only famous for jam but which was the birthplace of François de Guise who took Calais from the English in 1558, and of two of Napoleon's marshals – Exelmans and Oudinot. The Old Pretender retired to Bar-le-Duc after the Treaty of Utrecht. Yet, despite all this history, Bar-le-Duc seems to depend for its fame mostly on jam.

For the *fromage* Bar-le-Duc heat some water biscuits in the oven and serve with cream cheese and either quince jam, gooseberry jam or rhubarb jam, or, if you are a purist, with red-currant jam or jelly.

If you like the idea of gooseberry sauce with mackerel, all you have to do is to stew the gooseberries in water with a little sugar, blend them and add a pinch of nutmeg; and remember that this dish in French is not called *maquereau aux groseilles à maquereau* but *maquereau à l'anglaise* which may explain why one never comes across it in a French restaurant.

But why waste so much time on rhubarb and gooseberries when the fruit of the month must surely be raspberries? There are few things in the world which are more delicious than raspberries and cream or raspberry ice cream made with fresh cream, although I must admit that one day I am going to make a raspberry charlotte and I will use Mapie de Toulouse-Lautrec's recipe.

Soak the sponge fingers in Kirsch which has been diluted with water and line a souffle dish with them. Fill the centre with half the raspberries and cover with a further layer of biscuits before adding the remainder of the raspberries and a final layer of biscuits. Place a saucer and a weight on the dish and keep in the refrigerator over-night. Serve the charlotte turned out with a thin *crème anglaise* poured over it.

Crème anglaise is, of course, an affected way of saying "custard" and as I write I am reminded of Fowler's warning about the use of French in his *Modern English Usage*: "Display of superior knowledge is as great a vulgarity as display of superior wealth – greater indeed . . ." But I expect that most people who read about food know what a *crème anglaise* is and although a spade should usually be called a spade there is no doubt that the word custard conjures up terrible things in most people's minds, although I was deeply shocked to discover that one of my French friends used to buy custard powder in England to take back to France.

July Wines

Fortunately, the good Lord has arranged things so that nobody can eat tomato salad all the year round unless she has them specially flown from the southern hemisphere. For my own part, I would be perfectly happy to eat nothing but vegetable soup and bread every day for lunch, at any rate in the winter. A good, thick vegetable soup as a meal in itself (I am not talking about soup as a first course, which has been discussed already) can be accompanied by any wine ever made, the richer the better. But the tomato salad and Mozzarella cheese diet defies any clear drinking policy. It has never been inflicted on me and I suspect is is the sort of lunch which women eat when they are alone, or entertaining some woman friend. If they are putting anchovies with their Mozzarella – an excellent thing to do – water is probably the best drink, since concentrated anchovies have a terrible effect on wine. But if I find myself condemned to such a diet, no doubt in punishment for some grossness or other, I shall use the opportunity to explore as many French country reds as I can find. Many small wine merchants springing up in England specialize in this field, dealing in a variety of light, easy drinking reds in the 'B'–'C' price range. They seldom have much nose and often taste like a stronger wine which has had water added, but they are refreshing and easy to drink. An area which few English drinkers have explored, except those who have summer residences there, covers south-western France from the Dordogne to the Pyrenees.

Among the *vin de pays* of this region, there is none which is remotely nasty. The best I have discovered come from the Côtes du Tarn, the Côtes de Gascogne, whose whites, too, seem to be getting better with every year that passes, the Côteaux de Quercy, which specialize in a light Beaujolais style from the Gamay grape, and the Vins de Pays de la Dordogne, served by all the meaner summer exiles from Hampstead and Islington in their country cottages along the valley of the Lot.

Few of these wines are to be found on the lists of London wine merchants, although I have found a respectable Côtes du Tarn in the 'A'/'B' range on Sainsbury's shelves. Traditionally, it was reckoned that cheap wine of this sort was not worth the excise duty extracted impartially on all wines, regardless of price. But one sees more and more of the area's AOC wines creeping in – partly as the result of people holidaying in the area.

Most famous of these is Bergerac, cheaper than anything entitled to a Médoc label and often better. Generous hosts in the Dordogne serve Bergerac, mean ones serve Gaillac which is not as good, although perfectly good enough for drinking in France. There is excellent near-claret also being made nowadays in the Entre-Deux-Mers and even better comes from the Côtes du Frontonnais, to the north of Toulouse. This wine is at its best after three or four years in bottle, and, miraculously, can be brought at that age without much difficulty. The best Frontonnais comes from the village of Villandric, where producers tell me they have a big export market in Britain, although I have never seen it here, so goodness knows where it all goes. I imagine it disappears among these small importers who are springing up like mushrooms all over the countryside.

In twenty-five years of trying I have not yet found a good wine from Cahors, and feel people should be warned against it. For some reason it continues to enjoy a high reputation, although I have never met anyone who claims to have drunk a good bottle. The theory is that you should drink it very, very old. The oldest bottle I have ever found was a

1977 drunk in 1982 in a very expensive restaurant in Cahors, and I still thought it pretty foul. I am certainly not prepared to take up good cellar space with this unpleasant liquid on the off-chance that something wonderful will happen to it. The same is true to a lesser extent of the red wines of Madiran, although these are less nasty when young. For those who have ample cellar space and not too much money to fill them with, but who share my obsession that the pound is going to collapse in about five years' time and leave us unable to buy even the dregs of the Common Market Wine Lake, I would re-commend two red wines from the Rhône: Cornas, in the north, and Gigondas, in the south. These two really do improve with age for anything up to twenty years, and can be bought without difficulty in the 'C'/'D' range.

South-western France also provides some little known and unusu-ally cheap dessert wines to go with all the fruit dishes which are recommended for July. The point about these sweet wines, as I never tire of pointing out, is that they go wonderfully well with anything that is not *too* sweet, and even better with fruit which is a little sharp. Raw sugar does nothing to harm them, but the sweeter effect achieved by cooked sugar certainly does, removing much of the sweetness of the wine until, in extreme cases, you are left drinking something which tastes like a dry semillon from Australia. This is a tremendous waste of all the time and effort which go into making these sweet wines. For instance, my wife's fruit salad of orange and grapefruit slices with mint – which is absolutely delicious – goes very well with Sauternes or any other sweet dessert wine even after you have smothered it in sugar. But a commoner fruit salad, of orange slices with caramellised sugar broken over it, which she used to serve until she realized how many others were doing so, completely destroys any wine – even, I should guess, champagne. Rhubarb also destroys wine for reasons which I do not understand, but which may be something to do with iron.

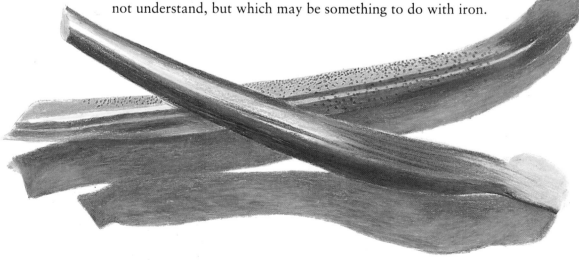

There can be no doubt that the best sweet wine in the world comes from Barsac and the rest of Sauternes, but it is becoming rather expensive. My own view is that it is foolish to serve a really good old vintage Sauternes – say a '67 or a '71 – with anything but a dry biscuit or at most a sliver of some very mild cheese, as one does not really want anything else to interfere with the taste. Incidentally, one can easily make one bottle do eight or even ten people, since nobody really wants to drink a lot. After more than one and a half glasses the palate is overwhelmed by the sweetness and the throat begins to burn. This rather reduces the cost of the luxury – and it is a luxury, in my experience, which guests greet with cries of delight, since so few people serve dessert wines nowadays.

But the younger Sauternes are a different matter. My own feeling is that a Sauternes has two lives. On one occasion I had dinner in Paris as a guest of Steven Spurrier's Académie du Vin, where they served a 1976 Yquem. Next morning I flew back to London for luncheon with Corney and Barrow, the City wine merchants, where, at the end of the meal, they served an Yquem from the classic and ancient vintage of 1947. Both wines were utterly delicious but they were totally different – the depth, weight and almost slightly burned taste of the older wine contrasting with the knockout freshness and zip of the younger – and for the life of me I could not decide afterwards which I had enjoyed the more. Under those circumstances, it occurs to me that it might be a bit of a waste of time to keep these magnificent wines for anything up to fifty years before drinking them, although I do not wish to be didactic on the subject.

In any case, one drinks wines of this quality nowadays only as a guest of wine merchants. Cheaper substitutes for all but the very best Sauternes can be found across the river at Loupiac and Sainte Croix-du-Mont. I may already have mentioned a Loupiac called Château Les Roques 1983 which had every characteristic of a first-class Sauternes except that it cost less than a quarter the price of the humblest classified example. Another bargain in dessert wines comes from the village a few miles south of Bergerac called Monbazillac. Although I *think* I might be able to distinguish a Monbazillac from a Sauternes, as it tends to be a trifle rougher, it is still a magnificently made sweet wine, even in a poor year, and would be greeted with rapture by most guests.

There is a small cult following for the sweet 'n' sour dessert wines of the Loire, made from the Chenin Blanc grape, but I tend to leave them to their devotees, although I was once given a wonderful and ancient Bonnezeaux by Robin Yapp which made me suppose there might be something in it all. And I have heard wonderful things of the *vin de paille* made in the Jura, but no wine merchant in England has ever thought to bribe me with some, and in fact I have never heard of a British wine merchant selling it. Imperial Tokay and Tokay Escenzia, from Hungary, once the treat of Russian Grand Dukes, is now drunk almost exclusively by English wine merchants, although occasionally a bottle comes up at Christies. (The Hungarian state monopoly in Tokay is handled by Coleman's of Norwich.) But to all intents and purposes the only dessert wine worth drinking comes from the Bordeaux region. Italian efforts in this direction centre around the muscat grape, but add up to nothing but a pale imitation of the Rhône's Beaumes de Venise – a wonderful wine in the 'D'/'E' range but scarcely for drinking with food. As I have already said, another excellent Moscatel comes from Fonseca in Setubal – it is also slightly cheaper – but the same objection applies.

What I miss in summer dessert courses is marmalade. There is scarcely a winter pudding ever invented which is not improved by marmalade. However, for those, like me, who pine without it, I recommend a Cypriot liqueur which tastes of nothing but marmalade of the very best Oxford variety made liquid. It is called Filfar and is wonderfully cheap in Cyprus, but horribly expensive in the few Soho shops which stock it.

AUGUST

I have seen jolly decent English families setting out on holiday, the boots of their cars filled with packets of cornflakes, jars of Marmite and bottles of salad cream. Some even go so far as to take marmalade, tea, lavatory paper and tins of baked beans. For all I know the occasional pallid sliced loaf may have crossed the Channel to blush beside its French counterpart. One of the main reasons for going abroad instead of to the Lake District or Cornwall is presumably because abroad is different so I am always puzzled by attempts to make it as like as possible to England. In Burma there are cottages built by the British in the hill stations which only go to show that they have always been keen on taking their salad cream and Marmite with them.

Unfortunately, partly thanks to the British, abroad is not nearly so different as it used to be. All the fresh pasta available in London nowadays must, however faintly, diminish the pleasure of eating it in Florence or Torcello. If you look hard enough you can probably find a tin of baked beans in Karachi or a packet of cornflakes in Lima, although I admit that you might have difficulty in finding a jar of Marmite in France. Try telling your children that "tea" in France consists of a couple of lumps of bitter chocolate and a piece of bread. The combination is delicious and any self-respecting child who has once tasted it will be happy to go without Marmite for a mere fortnight, if not for longer.

Shopping in France is no longer any more expensive than it is in England provided you don't want butter with everything or a leg of lamb every day. Besides which it is a treat to shop somewhere else for a change. I have been shopping regularly in France every summer for over twenty years now and nothing on earth would persuade me to take a single item of food there with me. Nor can I see any good reason for taking groceries to Italy, Greece, India or anywhere else I have ever been to. I have never, of course, been on a polar expedition or a test of endurance up the Amazon.

To return to France, there are one or two things not to buy, as for instance their vacuum-packed ready-peeled new potatoes which I have already mentioned. The French don't differentiate as carefully as we do between new and old potatoes but the big yellow potatoes which are on sale throughout the summer are perfectly delicious. There is no need to improve on them. Neither would I bother to buy their fat, white asparagus.

One thing about the French is that they seem to appreciate their fruit and vegetables as they come into season. For weeks on end they will buy Cavaillon melons and peaches and how right they are to do so. Who wants a frozen raspberry when they can have a fresh melon? Like a crab, a good melon should be heavy and you should be able to smell if a Cavaillon or Charentais melon is ripe.

For those who don't want to spend their entire holiday bent over the kitchen stove, France is the place to be. Regional dishes can be bought freshly cooked from a good *charcuterie* or *rôtisserie* – with a deposit on the dish which is often worth keeping. So you can buy Cassoulet in the Languedoc, *tripe à la mode de Caen* in Normandy, Coq Berrichon in Bourges, and so forth. Indeed you can buy a thousand other ready-made dishes from *écrevisses* to stuffed tomatoes, *lapin aux pruneaux* and *coq au vin*.

But, personally, I prefer to stuff my own tomatoes, peppers, courgettes and aubergines. None of these vegetables is expensive in France in the summer. For the stuffing, melt an onion and some chopped garlic in oil, add minced pork bought from the charcutier, and brown it. Put the mixture in a bowl and add salt, pepper, herbs, breadcrumbs, a beaten egg, a little red wine, and the pulp of the tomatoes and some chopped mushrooms. Stuff the vegetables, put them in a flat dish with a little olive oil and cook them in the oven for about an hour.

Because vegetables are inexpensive, ratatouille is another delicious thing to be made. In French supermarkets you can even buy a bag of mixed vegetables especially designed for ratatouille. One of the secrets of a good ratatouille is to cook it slowly for a long time – over an hour. Do not use too many tomatoes or it will be very runny. A first-class ratatouille is as they say "a meal in itself". In fact it is several meals in itself since it is equally good re-heated or cold.

If you feel that you must have meat, why not buy some guinea-fowl? I have never been given guinea-fowl to eat in England but in France they are as easily obtainable as chickens. Joint your guinea-fowl and brown the pieces in fat, melt some sliced onions and brown some bacon. Blanch a large cabbage and in a deep oven-proof dish put layers of cabbage, onion, meat, bacon and cabbage again. Add stock, herbs and garlic and put the dish in the oven for an hour and a half. Serve with boiled potatoes.

As a guinea-fowl is a rather dry bird it is not at its best roasted, although generally speaking recipes which are suitable for pheasant are also suitable for guinea-fowl. They can be cooked in cider or served with peaches or stuffed in the following way:

Make a stuffing with a mixture of chicken livers, onion, sausage meat, a handful of breadcrumbs and, if you can find such a thing, a tin of truffle parings. I have always thought that black truffles – the Périgourdine variety were tasteless and overrated, particularly when added to pâté de foie gras, but my opinion of their worth was reversed once and for ever when I ate them in Michel Guérard's famous restaurant. There the truffles, which were presumably fresh, were served thinly sliced in a mysterious creamy sauce of their own and they were exquisite.

In any case chop the chicken livers and onions or shallots and melt them in butter. Add the sausage meat and brown slightly; remove from the heat and add the breadcrumbs, truffle parings and a beaten egg and season. When you have stuffed the bird – one guinea-fowl should feed four people – butter it and place it in a buttered oven-proof dish on a bed of sliced onion and carrots. Cook in the the oven for about half an hour before adding a glass of port and some stock. Cook for a further thirty to thirty-five minutes. Carve the birds and serve them with the strained sauce poured over them. They may be accompanied by a dish of baby beetroots or possibly by some young carrots.

If you are a very thorough cook you could replace the sausage meat with a homemade pork forcemeat. For this you should melt some chopped onions in butter, put them in a bowl and add some white breadcrumbs which have been soaked in stock, strained and from which as much of the liquid as possible has been squeezed. Add the minced pork, seasoning, garlic and the herbs of your choice.

If you take your holidays in France and wish really to go native, you can always spend your time in search of mushrooms – particularly if the season is rainy and there are some woods round about.

One year, at the end of August, we were staying with some French cousins in a small moated manor house in Burgundy. Our hosts were, as country hosts tend to be, disappointed by the drenching rain which greeted our arrival. They clearly wondered how on earth to entertain us although we were quite simply just happy to be there. By the end of the first afternoon of our visit the rain began to let up although the sky was still heavy and the countryside sodden, and so it was agreed that this was an ideal afternoon for mushrooming. Neither Bron nor I had ever before picked anything other than field mushrooms so the prospect of the outing was rather exciting. Dressed in borrowed mackintoshes and boots and armed with great baskets we set out to tramp through the soaking woods, certain that we were about to be initiated into a new secret. The woods, to our delight, were filled with mushrooms and by the end of the afternoon all our baskets were brimming. We had asked our French cousin which ones to pick and he had told us that they were all good. On our way home laden with our pickings we stopped in a café where the proprietor was a noted mushroom expert – just to check that we had not allowed a few stray poisonous things to infiltrate our pickings. My cousin would rather be safe than sorry.

"Ah bonjour, Monsieur," the patron rubbed his hands together eagerly. "Qu'est ce que vous avez là? De beaux champignons pardi."

The café was filled with country folk dressed like us in boots and macs, puffing at their Gauloises and bewailing the weather. They all gathered round to peer into our baskets and – with one accord – and to a man they and the patron burst into gales of hearty laughter. Every single one of our mushrooms was poisonous.

Since this experience I have personally given up any attempt at picking my own mushrooms. Even with the help of reference books the task seems impossible. I have two books which show entirely different pictures of the chanterelle mushroom – or the *hygrophoropsis aurantiaca* as it is otherwise known. This is a delicious mushroom and one which is often to be found in French markets in summer and autumn and it is a shame that it is not more easily available in England.

The most sought-after mushrooms apart from the chanterelle or girolle are probably the morel and the boletus – or as it is called in France the cèpe. For those with confidence in their own judgement, I am told that the woods in Surrey are filled with cèpes from late August onwards and I know people who gather them there regularly.

Having abandoned any hope of finding my own cèpes, I once bought vast quantities in a Paris shop and flew home with them to England. When I proudly opened my shopping and boasted of the delicious supper I was going to cook for my family, my younger daughter turned as green as Babar the Elephant when he ate a poisoned mushroom and said that nothing on earth would persuade her to eat such things as they were crawling with maggots.

"Nonsense," I said furiously, but as I spoke methought the wood began to move. There was no doubt about it. I had brought a heaving mass of maggots home from Paris. On further investigation, I discovered that the speed at which the boletus develops maggots once it has been picked is quite incredible. I have no explanation for this phenomenon but only know that now I can neither pick these mushrooms nor buy them.

There are of course a great many different types of boletus: the best of which and the one which is most frequently eaten is the *Boletus edulis* or the *cèpe de Bordeaux*. It grows in woods, mostly under oak or beech trees, and is unbelievably delicious. Some other varieties are also edible, but the well-named *Boletus satanus* should be avoided at all costs.

One August I visited a friend in south-west France to discover that her entire kitchen was filled with what I thought were *cèpes de Bordeaux* but she assured me that what she had been collecting from the near-by pinewoods were *faux-cèpes*. I could not help thinking that these mushrooms must have some other name besides "*faux-cèpes*" but no one was able to tell me what it was. On returning to England I consulted my guide to mushrooms and, having decided against the ludicrously named *Boletus impolitus*, I decided that what my friend had collected must have been *Boletus Badius* which are described as growing mainly under conifers and are said to be edible and good. We were given some of the great harvest and, although they did not match up to the *cèpes de Bordeaux*, they were certainly very good.

Like most mushrooms the cèpes should be gently cooked in butter and garlic and served with a sprinkling of chopped parsley or chervil. They are excellent as an accompaniment to roast pigeon. We often eat *pigeonneau aux cèpes* in a small restaurant which we go to in the Languedoc.

In France cèpes and chanterelles and so forth can easily be bought in tins. I have tried these tinned mushrooms and would never recommend them. They have no taste and a rather vile consistency.

If you are, like me, nervous of collecting your own mushrooms and you are still quite determined to go native while on holiday in France, wait until it has rained and then go out and collect your snails. Starve the snails in a box full of flour with a lid and weights on top for at least a week. Plunge the snails into boiling water, remove them from their shells and cut off the greater intestine which is an easily recognisable black bit at the end of the tail. Simmer the snails for about an hour in water or stock with a bouquet garni, a carrot and an onion, drain them and return them to their shells with some garlic butter. Heat them quickly in a hot oven.

The best snails to use are the big *escargots de Bourgogne* which can incidentally also be found in England. I often come across them in my garden. But in the South of France people tend to make do with small whitish ones known as *petit gris* which can be found there in abundance. These are often served with chopped bacon and onion fried in fat and poured into the shell of the snail which has been prepared as described. Sometimes the snails are served out of their shells in a sauce made from the fried chopped bacon and onion to which a sprinkling of flour has been added and a glass or two of white wine. But, when all is said and done, I would always prefer to stick to the *escargots de Bourgogne* with garlic butter.

Once we went to a party in France known as an *escargolade*. It was a summer party and a huge barbecue was set up in the garden. On the grill, hissing and oszing, were hundreds of snails. Our hosts assured us that the snails, like St Lawrence, were being grilled alive. By co-incidence St Lawrence was the patron saint of the village where we were and the following day the villagers were due to celebrate his feast day.

There are several Saint Lawrences, one of whom succeeded St Augustine as Archbishop of Canterbury in 604, but the one of whom we treat was martyred in Rome in 258. According to the parish priest who preached to us the following day, St Lawrence was a man blessed with a remarkable sense of humour. Halfway through his ordeal by burning, he asked the executioner to turn him over as he was already "done" on one side. I do not suppose that the squeaks which rose from the army of snails on the grill had anything to do with humour but I rather hoped that they had nothing to do with pain either. I imagine that snails are probably too stupid to suffer pain and I believe that, unlike St Lawrence, they do not have an immortal soul and so could have had absolutely nothing to gain from their anguish.

Another thing which struck me about those snails was that, if they were being cooked alive, no one had removed the greater intestine. However that may be, the *escargolade* was a great success and we all managed to overcome our pity as we fell greedily on the poor snails which were dipped into an aioli before being eaten.

Another dish which I seem to associate with the month of August is rabbit – by which I do not mean wild rabbit but tame rabbit or *lapin de chou*. Before the introduction of myxamatosis, when I was a child just after the war, there were so many rabbits in the fields around our house that we must have eaten rabbit at least two or three times a week, so that the tendency was to think, oh no, not rabbit again. I never remember, in those days, eating tame rabbit, but now things have rather changed. A wild rabbit in a pie is a rare treat whereas the supermarkets are all filled with frozen tame rabbits most of which seem to have been flown in from China. I do occasionally buy this rabbit although not very often, but in August when I am in France I buy freshly killed tame rabbit from the market or from a neighbouring farmer.

These rabbits are quite unlike wild rabbits with a far milder taste, but they have a succulence all their own and are, to my mind, at their best served *à la moutarde*. There are various recipes for this dish but the simple one which I have always used is invariably greeted with cries of delight by my French and English friends alike, not to mention my family for whom it is a great favourite.

Butter a flat fire-proof dish and lay the jointed rabbit in it. Cover the pieces of rabbit in Dijon mustard and place a knob of butter on each piece. Cook in a fairly hot oven for about an hour, basting from time to time. When the rabbit is cooked remove it to another dish and stir a good half pint of cream into the juices. Pour this sauce over the rabbit and serve immediately with boiled potatoes, with a green salad to follow.

August is really rather a depressing, flowerless month. In England the leaves hang heavy and dusty-looking on the trees and the weather rarely comes up to expectation, but with *lapin à la moutarde* and the occasional *escargolade* there is nothing to fear.

August Wines

There are sound historical reasons why the English have always drunk less good French wine in France than they do in England – at any rate, since the war, which is as far as my memory goes. In my youth, foreign exchange was limited to some joke sum like £20 per person per year. I seem to remember that the Labour government reintroduced currency control at a similar absurd level after the devaluation in 1967. This meant that Englishmen abroad were always slumming it. Making a virtue of necessity, English travellers pretended to find some quasi-mystical quality in the horrid rough *vins de pays* – much nastier then than it is now – which economic circumstances forced them to drink:

> O for a beaker full of the warm South
> Full of the true, the blushful Hippocrene
> With beaded bubbles winking at the brim
> And purple-stained mouth.

There are still Englishmen who yearn for this blushful Hippocrene, or claim to do so. In my childhood we summered at my grandmother's house in Portofino, where we were served with a white wine made on the property. Even at that tender age, I identified it as one of the foulest beverages imaginable, but it seems to have established a sort of norm among some of my cousins, who also summered there, so that they now quite definitely prefer bad wine to good.

During those years of stringency it was quite normal for English hosts abroad to expect their guest to buy the wine and other drinks, explaining that currency control made them unable to do so. I know of at least one villa in the South of France where this convention still applies. The host does not seem to have noticed that currency control was abolished many years ago. Yet to expect guests in England to supply their own drink would be thought eccentric to the point of insanity. Mean people think it somehow aristocratical to slum it when they are abroad.

A second reason why Englishmen always drink cheaper wine in France than they do in England is that much of their eating is done in restaurants, and French restaurants, no less than English ones, expect to make a huge profit on classic vintage wine. As in England, it really is no joke to have to pay £25 for a bottle of wine in a restaurant which one could drink from one's own cellar for £7 or £8. And few Englishmen with holiday homes in France care to keep a cellar, since it is almost certain to be burgled when they are not there.

Another reason for not drinking the classic French wines in French restaurants is that all except the very best – those that make a speciality of their wine cellar, or those with at least two stars in Michelin – not only over-charge scandalously for their vintage wines but also offter only the wine from the poorest years. This may mean that they have drunk the best years themselves, or it may confirm what I suspect, that very few Frenchmen (outside the trade) know anything about wine. The best vintages are all snapped up by Americans, English, Dutch, Belgians, Germans and Japanese, leaving the unsaleable stuff to be bought by French restaurateurs at what they think are bargain prices. Perhaps because of drinking the production of off-years, the French also tend to drink their classic wines far too young, so even if they happen to have a bottle from a good year – a Bordeaux '83 or '82, for instance (the '75s, still too young to drink are considered really old wines by most French restauranteurs) or an '83 Burgundy or Rhône it will taste pretty nasty.

So all the pleasant dishes proposed by my wife as suitable for eating in France will be accompanied by whatever is the best local wine, regardless of whether it is particularly suitable for that dish or not. Until recently, an easy way to find out the best local wines was to look up the nearest starred restaurant in Michelin, where local wines were listed after the restaurant's specialities, but I have noticed that fewer restaurants do this nowadays. They have observed how tourists – especially the English – will always go for the cheap local wine rather than the expensive rubbish the wine waiter wants to sell them. By the same token, it is foolish to ask the wine waiter for his advice on the best local wine. He will always recommend the most expensive and pretentious, which, in the case of reds, will always be too young to drink and usually quite nasty. That is your punishment for not ordering his undrinkable Romanée-Conti 1975 at two thousand

francs, his Léoville-Poyferré 1968 at eight hundred or his Château Lafite 1965 at two thousand, five hundred francs.

A final reason for not drinking the great wines of France while in that country is that it is almost impossible to find a wine merchant – outside Paris and the great centres of Bordeaux, Beaune and Lyons – who sells them, except in the year or two years after their production. Many smart *épiceries* in the provinces will offer you really remarkable wines, like Château Pichon-Lalande 1982 or 1983, which might taste wonderful in ten or fifteen years' time, but would taste horrible now even if they had not been standing on the shelves for six months waiting for some poor mug to pay three hundred francs for them.

In my own part of France we drink Fitou – a good powerful wine made from the Carignan grape, which is aged eighteen months in cask and eighteen in bottle before being sold at 16–20 francs, and the grey-pink Listel which I have already mentioned as being no good in England, but which goes down a treat in France at 12 or 14 francs a bottle. Other good and even cheaper reds come from Minervois and the huge Corbières region, but there is no white wine worth drinking until you get considerably further north. The nearest approach to a decent white wine is called *vin vert de Roussillon* about which I can only say that it is better than *vinho verde* from Portugal.

Really mean Englishmen will buy the nasty wine which comes in plastic litre bottles at four francs the litre at all the big grocery chains and make the same noises over it they used to make over the *gros rouges qui tâchent*, imagining that they are being truly French and ethnic and going native with a vengeance. Such people are to be despised more than they are to be pitied, because this plastic plonk, although I suspect it is full of chemicals and probably unhealthy, does not actually taste too nasty nowadays, and is certainly much less nasty than the farmers' old *gros rouge*. But it is not particularly nice, either, and people who insist on drinking it when they are in France are missing out on one of the greatest pleasures of life, for the sake of a few francs.

Large areas of France, of course, do not make any wine at all, so Englishmen do not have the option of choosing a local product and congratulating themselves on their wisdom and *savoir-faire*. Most of the north is wineless, and so is a large chunk of central France often known as La France Bossue. In fact it would be possible to walk from the Italian border a little east of Nice to Calais in the far north-west of France without seeing a single vine.

I do not seriously think I would advise Englishmen to drink cider when in Normandy, although they make some very good commercial sparkling cider there, if you can get away from the bogus *pots* of old farmhouse cider with which Norman innkeepers sometimes tempt us. It is certainly better than equivalent cider from Somerset, Devon or Hereford, and as good as the best from Merrydown, in Sussex. Nor would I advise them to drink the still white and red wines of Champagne, which are villainously over-priced and in my experience pretty nasty. Those finding themselves in a French restaurant where there is no local wine would be well advised to stick to Beaujolais, which does not suffer from being drunk young, or white Sancerre, which is ubiquitous. Slightly cheaper than Beaujolais is red Bourgueil, which is nearly always good, or a Gamay de Touraine, which has been getting better and better. Rosé from Provence is now to be found on nearly every restaurant wine list in the north of France, and seldom tastes too bad. Another of the pleasures of spending a certain amount of time in France every year is to reflect on all those splendid French wines which are quietly maturing in one's cellars at home, back in England.

SEPTEMBER

In September the fishmongers' shops begin to be filled with mussels again and as the 'R' comes back into the month so do oysters become available.

Not one of my cookery books gives any useful advice on how to open an oyster. Mrs Beeton goes so far as to say, "Do not try to open them yourself." I have seen men pale at the prospect of opening oysters and I have seen them drip with blood like Coriolanus after the taking of Corioli as they struggle manfully against apparently unequal odds.

Then one day I was walking with my elder daughter in the market place of a small town in south-west France when I saw a stall piled with nothing but oysters. The stall holder was exhorting us loudly to buy his wares. I explained that I loved oysters but that as neither my daughter nor I could open them there was little point in our buying them. Then and there he showed us what to do and, delighted, we bought some oysters which we took home and opened later that evening with no trouble whatsoever.

Hold the oyster in your left hand with the joint towards your wrist and the flatter side uppermost. Divide it mentally into three and insert your knife into the side of the shell nearest to you at a point which is two-thirds along the shell towards the joint. This will damage the muscle which allows the oyster to remain tightly closed and you will be able to open the shell easily by inserting your knife in the front end.

Really I think that oysters are such a tremendous delicacy that there is little point in messing around with them and they should be served *au naturel* with lemon and if you like it a little tabasco sauce. Having said that, I do seem to remember a remarkable dish of poached oysters served in a creamy sauce on a bed of seaweed which I once ate in a restaurant in La Rochelle, and then there is a recipe in *The Gentle Art of Cookery* for oysters wrapped in bacon, fried and served with a squeeze of lemon on fried bread.

More recently I spent a week-end near Bayeux in Normandy. The occasion was my mother's birthday – she was entering a new decade – and to celebrate the event she, my brother, his wife, their three children, Bron, myself and our four children spent a gastronomic week-end all together in an eighteenth-century château which is now a hotel. The month was September, the weather was fine, and it was a glorious end to what had until then been a rather grey summer. The gastronomic delights were equally appreciated by one and all, so that even my youngest niece, aged seven, competed on equal terms with the rest of us, insistent that the entire menu be translated for her and eagerly gobbling up the delicacies which came her way. No nonsense about "fish fingers" in that family.

Of all the wonderful things which were put in front of us that week-end we agreed unanimously that the very best was a poached fillet of salmon rolled around an oyster and served with a *beurre blanc* sauce. It was certainly as near perfection as anything I have ever eaten.

My brother, who is an enthusiastic not to say impatient cook, hurried home from the week-end and by 8.30 on Monday morning he was trying to buy a calf's head from a butcher in Surrey. The butcher's boy informed my brother apologetically that in England calves' heads never left the slaughter houses. "E.E.C. regulations."

"Impossible," said my brother, "we have been eating calves" heads all week-end in France."

The butcher's boy, ever helpful, explained patiently that they don't have E.E.C. regulations over there.

My brother is not one to have his enthusiasms easily crushed nor his spirits dashed, so he forgot about the calf's head and made his way to the fishmonger. He was quite lucky really as my fishmonger and my butcher are both closed on Mondays. When he got there he discovered that the fishmonger was reluctant to fillet a salmon – my fishmonger suggests filleting the tail or (and this I think is the best idea) using sea trout – but my brother chose fillets of sole and swears that the end result was just as delicious as the original salmon. The fish fillet, then, should be wrapped around a raw oyster, tied and gently poached in salted water with an onion and some parsley.

A *beurre blanc* is a sauce which, as every cookery book will tell you, needs great care in the making. And all the cookery writers agree that the excellence of the end result makes the care worth while. Two shallots should be finely chopped and gently blanched in a tablespoon-ful of water, two tablespoons of vinegar with a little salt and pepper. Reduce the liquid to a third of its original quantity. Add the butter (6–7 ozs. cut into little bits) gradually, beating hard all the time with a metal whisk until it is well incorporated, frothy and white. The heat under the pan must be consistent (neither too hot nor too cool) for the butter to remain frothy and not become oily.

Although mussels can be delicious raw, they are, I think, usually
nicer cooked but I must admit to being rather lazy about cooking them
because of the enormous effort involved in cleaning them, and besides
it is risky to offer them to guests as some people are genuinely allergic
to them. There are people who have an odious habit of announcing
that they are allergic to anything they don't like such as parsnips or
beetroot or "cooked cheese", but one must believe that allergies to
shell fish are genuine. Perhaps other people like myself feel faint-
hearted at the prospect of scraping mussels and that is why they are so
popular in restaurants, where someone else has done the work.

To clean your mussels you should rinse them thoroughly in cold
water and then remove them from the water, scrape them and leave
them in a bowl without water. When you have scraped them all, run
the water over them, turning them over as you do so. Continue to
change the water until it remains clear. As you turn them round they
will be too frightened to open but, according to one French book, if as
you scrape them you place them one by one in still water they will open
and close again, thus trapping any dirt which is floating in the water.

Once you have cleaned the mussels *moules marinières* are easy to make. Put them in a pan with pepper, parsley, thyme and a couple of chopped shallots. Add two or three glasses of white wine and cook with the lid on the pan until all the mussels have opened. Strain the liquid from the mussels and add a large knob of butter to it. Boil rapidly to reduce. Pour the liquid over the mussels from which you have removed the beards and sprinkle with chopped parsley.

If you prefer your mussels *à la creme*, open them in the same way. Make a white sauce and, when it is boiling, pour it into a bowl in which you have whipped together an egg yolk and some cream, beating as you pour. Add either a pinch of curry powder, some cayenne pepper or perhaps a little saffron according to your taste. Add the mussels to the sauce with a little of the wine in which they have cooked. Sprinkle with chopped parsley.

Moules farçies are a marvellous way of cooking mussels. Open the mussels in white wine as you would for *moules marinière*. Throw away the empty halves of the shells and arrange the others in a flat fire-proof dish. Mash some butter with garlic, thyme and some chopped

parsley. Put a little of the butter mixture on each mussel and sprinkle with fine white breadcrumbs. Place the dish under the grill until the butter has melted and the breadcrumbs have browned.

September not only brings mussels and oysters but, as the summer draws to an end, there seems to be everywhere a glut of vegetables. For those with their own gardens there are almost too many. The happy housewife may well enjoy endless afternoons slicing beans to be either salted or frozen. That done, she will turn her hand to green tomato chutney, apple chutney, marrow chutney and possibly most delicious of all – marrow jam.

Others who have no time – or at any rate no time for husbandry – along with the plain greedy and those who despise the frozen bean will concentrate their minds on how to eat their way through this mountain of lettuces, tomatoes, courgettes, cucumbers, marrows, peppers and so forth. I might mention at this point that in fact ratatouille does not suffer in the least from being frozen.

So now is the time to invite your friends to supper in an attempt to put the cornucopia to good use.

By September you have probably had enough lettuce or cucumber soup so you will be searching your mind for something different – you will even be trying to find a new way of using tomatoes. So why not make a tomato tart? Fill your pre-cooked pastry case with a layer of béchamel flavoured with tomato purée and thyme. Cover this with finely sliced tomatoes and return to the oven for about ten minutes. Sprinkle with chopped anchovies and black olives before serving. There are other ways of making tomato tarts but this is certainly one of the best and one which is invariably greeted with cries of joy in my house.

To my mind one of the most under-rated vegetable dishes is braised lettuce. The lettuce should be blanched before being placed in a buttered dish on a bed of onions, covered with meat stock and cooked gently in the oven for some forty-five minutes. These are delicious served with boiled gammon.

A lettuce is of course also used when cooking *petits pois à la française*, and there can be no doubt that the older, fatter pea is far happier when baked *à la française* with butter, onion, bacon, salt, pepper, a little sugar water and chopped lettuce.

The Gentle Art of Cookery contains an excellent recipe for what is called lettuce à l'espagnole in which halved, blanched lettuces are baked with a little stock, cloves and an onion under a layer of bacon

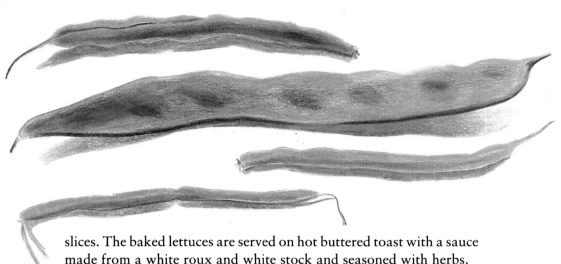

slices. The baked lettuces are served on hot buttered toast with a sauce made from a white roux and white stock and seasoned with herbs.

There seems to be a generally held opinion that courgettes are superior to marrows. Perhaps this is because of the rarity value they once had but, now that they are to be found in the shops all the year round, I feel that their charms have faded. Besides, they have a nasty way of turning up in greasy little heaps in every second-rate Italian restaurant. In any case I have, on the whole, come to prefer a beautiful smooth marrow.

At this time of year I tend to stuff my vegetable marrows with minced pork, chopped onion, herbs, seasoning, garlic, breadcrumbs, an egg, a drop of red wine, a chopped tomato and some mushrooms. The onion should be melted in fat and the meat browned first. The stuffed vegetable is then baked with a little olive oil for about an hour.

Marrow is also good when cut into small cubes, rolled in flour and deep fried. A nice addition to plain, steamed marrow is a thick coating of grated Gruyère cheese.

Then of course there are French beans and runner beans, both of which are perfectly excellent cooked in the simplest possible way, or made into a salad with tomatoes.

A slightly more unusual way of cooking French beans (not perhaps runner beans) is to put them in a pan with some diced bacon and chopped peeled tomatoes, cover them with a little stock and cook them slowly for about an hour.

One of the most welcome vegetables at any time of year is spinach, and despite its distinctive taste and texture it seems to be remarkably versatile. A handful of chopped spinach in a stew is an excellent addition. Then there are all the well-known dishes like spinach soup, spinach and bacon salad, spinach and avocado salad, pancakes stuffed with spinach, spinach soufflé and, perhaps most glorious of all, *sformato di spinaci*. A *sformato* is a kind of steamed soufflé which when it is cooked is turned out onto a dish and served with, for instance, a tomato sauce or a cream sauce. Elizabeth David gives an excellent recipe for a *sformato* in her *Italian Food*. She also recommends making it with peas and French beans, spinach or even fennel. A certain amount of trouble should be taken in making a *sformato* but the result is more than worth it.

The *sformato* is made by mixing some cooked, puréed or finely chopped spinach into a thick béchamel sauce to which you add seasoning, chopped ham and a handful of grated Gruyère. Stir in the yolks of eggs and then the stiffly beaten whites. Steam in a buttered soufflé dish with the cover on the pan for about an hour.

Another way of using spinach is to make spinach croquettes. Make a thick béchamel sauce and allow it to cool. Add to the cold sauce some cold, finely chopped spinach, a pinch of nutmeg, salt, pepper and a handful of grated Parmesan and the beaten yolks of two eggs. When the mixture is completely cold divide it into croquettes which you dip in beaten egg and roll in breadcrumbs before cooking in hot oil.

Like tomatoes, spinach and many other vegetables such as onions, leeks and indeed courgettes can be used to make tarts – and excellent tarts at that.

A certain amount of myth is generally attached to the making of pastry. When I was first married and began to cook – over twenty years ago now – I was convinced that I could never make good pastry so I used frozen pastry which was considerably less palatable than it is now. Eventually pride took the upper hand and I decided that I had to make the effort. There are born pastry cooks among whom I do not number, but after much trial and error I have finally settled for my own way which takes all of five minutes and, as I am generally in a hurry, I do not even let the pastry stand before rolling.

Always use just over half the quantity of fat to flour. This makes the pastry more crumbly. For a savoury quiche or tart, use half margarine and half lard, for a sweet tart use margarine and a dessertspoonful of sugar. I only use granulated sugar, never caster. Since those far-off days I have acquired a Magimix – a truly wonderful machine which is invaluable in a thousand ways. It even makes pastry but I must admit that, if I want my pastry to be particularly good, I will still make it by hand. There are of course also times which require an especial effort when, for instance, the making of flaky or puff pastry requires close attention to Constance Spry or Mrs Beeton – but these occasions are few and far between.

The most elegant way to present any kind of tart is to cook it in a loose-bottomed case. There is a claustrophobic and somewhat sweaty look about them when they are served in those specially designed china dishes with crinkly edges. These dishes seem to suggest wedding lists and London stores more than honest greed.

Most cookery books fail to point out that, unless pastry cases are blind-baked, they are almost invariably soggy. Personally I never cook a quiche or tart of any kind without blind-baking the pastry first. Everyone knows how to make a quiche, but few really succeed. I think that one of the nastiest things available can be a slab of cold quiche as it is served in any number of pubs and wine bars. If the eggs are well whipped with a little thyme, cream, salt, pepper and a handful of grated cheese (preferably Gruyère or Emmenthal) before being poured over the bacon and onion mixture, and if the quiche is left long enough in the oven, the eggs will rise like a soufflé and go brown on top. Eaten hot this is delicious, but cold it becomes flat and too dry.

There is a particularly good recipe whereby a cheese soufflé mixture is baked in a pastry case. It is elegant and excellent served with just a green salad. I have tried a successful variation of this with a spinach soufflé mixture. These mixtures require fewer egg whites than an ordinary soufflé as there would be too much filling for the pastry case.

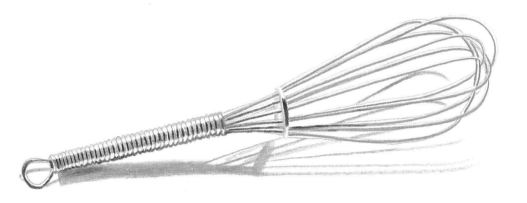

W H I S K

Many cookery books give a recipe for an onion tart but leeks can be just as good. Stew some chopped leeks in butter, make a thick white sauce, add two well-beaten eggs and the leeks, put the mixture in the pastry case, sprinkle with grated cheese and bake until the cheese is brown.

Of course you need not fill your pastry case with vegetables, you may prefer the idea of eggs or fish. Cook a pastry case and just as it is ready scramble some eggs with a little chopped ham, fill the pastry case and serve immediately. In summer time this recipe can be made substituting asparagus tips for the ham.

For a lobster or crab – or, rather less extravagantly, a prawn tart – fill the partly cooked case with a mixture of beaten eggs and cream into which you have put the fish. Sprinkle with grated cheese and return to the oven for ten to fifteen minutes. A good firm white fish could be mixed with the peeled prawns and replace the lobster or crab here.

Tarts served as pudding should never be overlooked. People are becoming lazier and lazier about making puddings which means that when one does appear it is all the more welcome. Apart from anything else, tarts are as decorative as any pudding so that, if by the end of the meal you feel you have had enough to eat, their sheer prettiness will tempt you to go on. For these tarts you should use a sweet pastry.

I have already talked about strawberry tarts which are among the very best and anyway strawberries are no longer in season in September, but a good apple tart runs a very close second. Make a purée of cooking apples – preferably Bramleys. Add a tablespoonful of dark marmalade to the purée and spread it over the bottom of the tart case. On top of the purée arrange dessert apples, peeled and sliced into half-moon shapes. Coat the apples with melted apricot jam. Put the tart in the oven until the dessert apples are cooked and serve cold with thick cream.

An even more delicious apple tart which is a little more trouble to make is a *tarte des Demoiselles Tatin*. This is an upside-down tart for which you must make a flaky pastry – a long job but one which is well worth the effort. Spread the bottom of a shallow cake tin with a layer of butter and cover this with a layer of sugar. Peel and core some cooking apples, slice them finely and arrange them in layers on top of the sugar and butter. Press down firmly and cover the apples with another layer of sugar and layer of butter. Roll out the flaky pastry which must have been left to relax and make a lid to cover the apples.

Press down firmly again and bake in a hot oven for thirty to forty minutes. When the tart is cooked, turn it out upside down on to a plate so that the apples which will be brown and slightly caramelized with a transparent look are uppermost.

For a pear tart, peel, halve and core the pears; poach them gently in water and sugar. Remove them from the liquid and allow the syrup to boil until it reaches the thread stage. Dissolve some red-currant jelly in syrup. Fill the ready cooked pastry case with *crème patissière* or some *frangipani* which is a *crème patissière* to which you have added crushed macaroons or ground almonds. Place the halved pears on the *frangipani* and coat with the red-currant syrup.

To make *crème patissière*, thoroughly whip three egg yolks with 125 grams of sugar and half a teaspoonful of vanilla essence. Add 50 grams of flour and $\frac{1}{3}$ litre of boiling milk. Return to the heat and boil, stirring all the while, until the *crème* has thickened.

With all this discussion of apples and pears and strawberries, let it not be forgotten that everybody loves a treacle tart and most people know how to make one, but I must mention that I sometimes make it with brown instead of white breadcrumbs and I find there is a definite improvement. One last tip, if you have any foreign friends you will find that they have probably never eaten treacle tart. Even my French friends are momentarily taken aback by this unexpected glory of English cooking.

September Wines

I have never decided what is the best wine to drink with oysters. In restaurants I generally drink what they call their house Chablis rather than their house hock – a rather thin, sharp Chardonnay rather than a thin, sharp Riesling. I feel in my bones that it would be a mistake to drink anything fuller or richer, although to tell the absolute truth I am not sure I have ever tried. The raw oyster – with or without lemon or tabasco – is such a strong and particular taste that it seems bound to find itself in conflict with anything richer than a village Chablis of rather a poor year. It is one of those rare occasions where wine should be the servant of food, rather than its wife or boon companion, serving in the office of salt to bring out the taste of the oyster rather than offering a concomitant pleasure of its own. At any rate, that is how I feel on this important subject.

If I am right, this may explain why so many people swear by Muscadet as the perfect companion to raw oysters (poached or warmed oysters are quite different, and would make a perfect foil for the richest Californian Chardonnay, not to mention a Montrachet or a Corton Charlemagne, so long as the sauce was not too creamy). There are some excellent Muscadets being made, notably by Sauvion & Fils whose Domaine de Bois Curé 1983 is my favourite, but even the best are pretty austere by the standards set elsewhere. However, many Muscadets served in London restaurants as their cheapest wine are so nasty that I feel it is an area best left alone, while the gooseberry-leaf flavour of the better Sauvignons – from Sancerre, Pouilly-sur-Loire and Graves – generally set themselves up in opposition to the wonderful salty, metallic taste of our native oysters from Colchester

and Whitstable – surely, although one hesitates to be too loud about it, the best in the world. Perhaps the best Muscadet is the answer but, truth to tell, we have oysters so infrequently at home (despite my wife's marvellous new skill in opening them) that I have never bothered to buy a Muscadet for the cellar.

Butter, although a wonderful substance, is an enemy to most wines, and fish served in a buttery – or even very creamy – sauce should be taken with a young white wine, whether Chardonnay or still better, Sauvignon, where the acid is still very much in evidence. Both Australian and Californian whites tend to be short on acid – I do not know why – and should be avoided, as should the innumerable cheap Italian and Languedoc whites, made from ignoble and largely unknown grapes, since they tend to be short on taste and fruit, although undeniably sharp. One has to be very careful indeed in choosing a white wine to accompany a good fish, in the first place not to drown the delicate taste of the flesh, in the second place because one notices the taste of the wine much more critically than usual. The easiest way out is to serve a sound German Kabinett of a good year – 1983 was wonderful – but I have noticed a definite reluctance among serious wine drinkers to interest themselves in good German wine since the English wine market became flooded with semi-sweet imitations of sugared-up Eurowine.

Moules marinière is a wonderful dish, but not one requiring a very serious wine. Standard red Côtes du Rhone is good enough, or one of the excellent Riojas shipped by Messrs Laymont and Shaw of Truro – Viña Alberdi is the lighter, in range 'C', Viña Ardanza is heavier in range 'D', or you could go a bomb on one of the Gran Coronas Reservas from Torres, in Penedes, at prices which start middle 'D' and climb just into the 'G' bracket with their older "Black Label". Spanish wines have the great advantage that they are aged before they reach the shops, and the Torres range is available nearly everywhere. The best Spanish wine I have ever drunk was an Imperial Gran Reserva 1970 from the Cia Vinicola del Norte de España at Haro but this is hard to find now. I have been told that the 1975 is as good, selling now (early 1986) at the very reasonable price of £5.75 from Laymont and Shaw.

Most of the dishes suggested for September go very well with a thick, heavy red wine, coarser than Burgundy or claret, which can absorb the sharpness in my wife's delicious tomato tart and might even smother the anchovies. I am thinking, of course, of old Châteauneuf du Pape but that is almost unprocurable unless you are prepared to lay it down. Loeb, of Jermyn Street, sometimes has some, but it is not cheap. A good substitute for old Châteauneuf is the junior wine from Beaucastel, called Cru du Coudelet and shipped by Chris Collins of Bibendum, in Regents Park Road, N.W.1; it can still be found in the 'C' range, ready for drinking after three years with many characteristics of the old stuff. Another excellent wine of this sort, although considerably more elegant, is the Lebanese wine which excites me so much from Serge Hochar at Château Musar.

Otherwise, the prospects for buying mature wine seem dim, unless you are prepared to take time off to taste and bid at Christie's or Sotheby's. One shop – Reid Wines, of Marsh Lane, Hallatrow, Bristol – specialises in old vintages, but its prices are quite high. For those who are prepared to lay down wine, but do not have enough money to buy the classic wines whose prices seem to leapfrog every year, I have three suggestions. The first is Gigondas, once part of the Côtes du Rhône Villages, now awarded its own *appellation*. The price of a new Gigondas hovers between 'C' and 'D'; after four years it is already good to drink, but I learned just how good Gigondas can be when I found a half-bottle of Jaboulet's 1967 example in the Escargot Restaurant, Greek Street recently. A superb wine, comparable to any Châteauneuf at twice or three times the price. The other two wines which I would recommend for laying down in a modest way should also be procurable in the 'C' range – Bandol, from Provence, and Domaine de Trevallon shipped by Robin Yapp. Both drink well after four or five years, and both taste like old wines, which is the important thing. I am also experimenting with laying down some Australian Cabernet Sauvignon – for some extraordinary reason these wines cost less to ship from Australia than claret costs to ship from Bordeaux – but obviously I will not be in a position to report on my experiment for another five years.

Finally, to repeat an earlier warning. My wife's delicious apple tart (with that magic touch of marmalade) is just about all right when accompanied by a Sauternes, but there is absolutely nothing you can drink with a treacle tart except cream.

OCTOBER

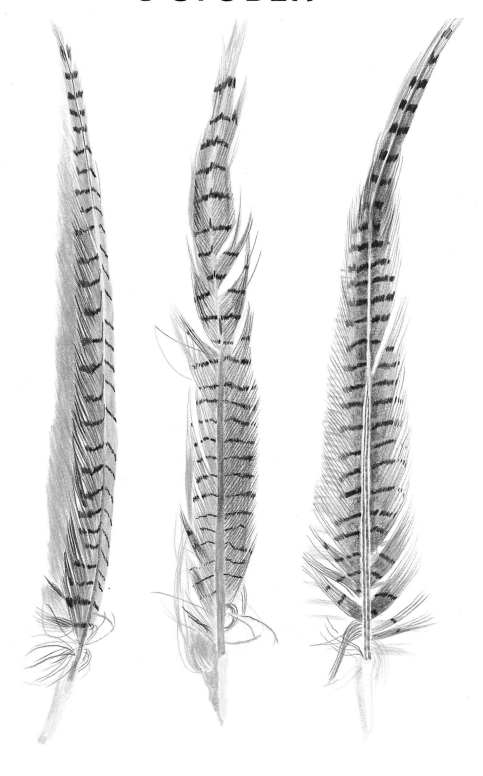

Throughout my childhood I hated shooting lunches. At home they all led to the fearful and inevitable moment when my father would announced that the children could join the beaters in the afternoon. Children enjoyed beating and it was good for them. In my experience children hated beating. Certainly the prospect of an afternoon to be spent wading through head-high, wet kale was enough to put even the greediest child off its lunch.

Not only did I hate the wet kale and the smell of it, but I was gun-shy, liable to bury my head in my arms and throw myself to the ground at the first sound of fire. Then there are memories of standing for hours in a blistering east wind waiting for the first tame pheasant to bite the dust, and longing for the daylight to fade.

All this really goes to show is that I am perhaps the last person to discuss shooting lunches. But there is no doubt that one is reminded of them in the autumn and I do remember a glorious hamper unpacked on the hill in Scotland out of which came huge round baps filled with fried eggs. The following day the baps had scrambled eggs in them and never have baps tasted better nor been more suited to the occasion.

One autumn I attended a shoot in France. There the day seemed to have been arranged in a far more practical way than is usual in England. Only a meagre snack at noon – mere hard-boiled egg and a petit-beurre biscuit. At six o'clock in the evening, famished, bathed and changed, we all sat round a huge table and ate a sumptuous dinner of quiche followed by roast mutton, cheese and caramel cream. Those canny French were not prepared to waste daylight hours eating when they could have been massacring God's innocent creatures. As a result, when the guns admired the bag, beautifully laid out at the end of the day, an amazing number of innocents had been sent to meet their maker since morning. The scene resembled nothing so much as the battlefield at Eylau.

There is no doubt that the traditional English heavy shooting lunch presents problems. The guns are hungry, yet if they eat too much and too well, they will be missing more birds than they should in the afternoon. As they tuck into their game pie which can be made with any combination of pheasant, wild duck, pigeon or whatever, the will is bound to weaken and they will want more and they will then find themselves hustled through their Stilton so as to leave time for the last drives before it grows too dark.

So the lunch must be speedily eaten, yet filling.

There is no reason why a good thick soup made from lentils, or split peas with bacon added, should not be served as the *plat de résistance*. This could be followed by cold meats, baked potatoes, a winter salad or chicory, beetroot and mâche.

A rich fruit cake is an excellent substitute for a pudding. If you don't care to make a fruit cake the tinned ones, available from high-class grocers and made with Guinness, are quite delicious. A tangerine makes a fine accompaniment to a piece of fruit cake.

Perhaps the most obvious dish to serve for hungry guns in winter is a good stew. When making a stew, many people follow recipes with fancy foreign names, but my advice to the cook is quite simple. Make sure you buy good quality meat and, with a sharp knife, rid it of every sinew and piece of fat. Brown the meat, garlic, onion and carrots in the best dripping you have. Duck fat is excellent. Flamber the meat – almost any alcohol will do. When there has been no brandy, I have used whisky. I must admit that I have never tried gin and would hesitate to do so. Cook your stew in good wine. Wine which has been open for days will ruin it. Add whatever root vegetables and herbs that you fancy – onions and carrots are essential, so I think is a turnip which will thicken the sauce. Celery is a good addition. Do not use flour. A little tomato purée will not go amiss, although too much will give a metallic flavour. Half a tin of tomatoes or two or three skinned and frozen tomatoes will also help to thicken the juices. Cook the stew slowly the day before serving it. Remove the fat from the top before reheating. If you plan to make dumplings – and everyone loves dumplings – make sure that you have more liquid than usual as it will reduce and thicken drastically.

Do not serve messy, lumpy mashed potato with stew. Fluffy boiled potatoes with a sprinkling of chopped parsley are not only less trouble, but are also far nicer.

And then of course one's mind naturally turns to game, and rabbits and pigeons which may not technically be regarded as "game".

As I have already remarked, when I was a child the Flopsy Bunnies of this world thrived. Despite the efforts of a few red-faced farmers with their guns and a furious Mr McGregor, the rabbit population grew. Then came the holocaust – and for years there was not a bunny in sight – perhaps an occasional, poor, swollen parody of the fierce, bad rabbit we loved to hate. It was during those years that we learned to put up with imported Chinese rabbits and, delicious though they may be *à la moutarde*, there is nothing to touch a wild rabbit.

Today the rabbit population is on the increase again and, according to recent information, rabbits have developed a very real immunity to myxomatosis. I find my sentimental attitude towards them has changed somewhat as I see them every night and morning playing on my lawn and as I consider the careless havoc they wreak in my flower-beds. But we do occasionally get one for the pot.

Old cookery books are full of recipes for rabbit. Mrs Beeton devotes no fewer than eight pages to rabbits, with recipes for rabbit soufflé and rabbit *à la minute*. *The Gentle Art of Cookery* advises you to fry your jointed rabbit gently in butter, then to pour melted butter and chopped parsley over it and to allow it to simmer for a few minutes before serving it in a silver dish.

I have an old housewife's manual dating back to the middle of the last century which advises me "to smother rabbits" – that is to truss and boil them and then to smother them with white onion sauce. All the same, I think that a rabbit pie is as good as anything. Brown the pieces of rabbit with a generous amount of chopped bacon and stew in a little white wine and stock with herbs and seasoning until the rabbit is tender. Remove the meat from the bones before covering with the pie-crust and cooking the pastry. Hard-boiled eggs are a welcome addition to a rabbit pie.

The awful thing about hare as far as I am concerned is that I can never look at it with pleasure since a jugged hare in a London restaurant some twenty odd years ago gave me acute food poisoning. But I am sure that the devotee of that rich and rather violent meat will have no difficulty in finding a recipe for jugging it.

Venison is, I suppose, just as rich as hare, but having had no quarrel with it I welcome it on the rare occasions when it comes my way. I don't particularly like it roast, but have from time to time cooked it according to a French recipe for wild boar whereby the meat is marinaded for twenty-four hours in red wine with a little oil, vinegar, a carrot, an onion, cloves, herbs, garlic and seasoning and cooked slowly in water or stock, a little of the marinade, carrots and herbs.

My old housewife's manual suggests boning the venison which is an exceptionally lean meat, flattening it out and spreading thin slices of fat mutton over it. Sprinkle the meat with herbs and spices and then roll it up tightly. Stew slowly for about three hours.

Many people in England believe that pheasant is at its best traditionally roasted with all the right accompaniments – home-made, paper-thin potato crisps, bread sauce, bacon, fried breadcrumbs, gravy and watercress salad. That is all very well but it is a bit tough on the poor cook-hostess. Preparing pheasant like this is rather like getting breakfast on time without burning the toast or cracking the egg or boiling the milk over. Incidentally I was taught to roast a pheasant upside down with plenty of bacon rashers over it and a little milk in the bottom of the pan. This prevents the bird from being too dry.

If you cannot face the hassle of properly presented roast pheasant, I would suggest cooking it as the French cook partridge or guinea-fowl – jointed, browned and stewed with layers of blanched cabbage, onion and bacon.

Or follow Mapie de Toulouse-Lautrec's excellent recipe for *faisan braisé aux pommes*. Brown the pheasant in a pan. Peel and slice the apples and brown them in butter without allowing them to cook. Put a layer of the apples in the bottom of the pan in which you have browned the pheasant. Put the pheasant on top of the apples and put more apples around the bird, season and add a little cinnamon. Mix the juice of half a lemon and a small glass of calvados with four ounces of cream and pour over the bird. Finally add some soaked sultanas or currants. Cover the pan and cook gently for about thirty-five minutes. Personally I think the raisins or currants are an unnecessary addition to what must surely be by origin a Norman dish. You can of course serve it quite simply *à la crème* which involves cooking it in the same way as above but using rather more cream and omitting the apples and Calvados. A sliced onion should be browned with the pheasant at the beginning.

I find that pigeons make a welcome change. They are delicious roast with a few stoned and peeled grapes inside them and served on croutons spread with a good liver pâté. A little damson cheese, or damson jam melted into the gravy, adds a thickness to the juices and a welcome bitter-sweet taste to the dark, rather heavy meat of the pigeon.

Should you find yourself with a glut of pigeons, insert a sharp knife down the breastbone of the birds, the feathers will then peel off and you will be able to remove each breast whole. Dispose of the rest of the bird and make a glorious stew of pigeon breasts. This should be cooked slowly and for quite some time as pigeon can be rather tough.

Pigeons can be cooked like duck with olives or they can be cooked in the traditional Languedoc way, with a stuffing made from their own livers, some breadcrumbs, garlic, parsley and thyme and bound with an egg. Brown the pigeons in goose fat if you have it – most households in the Languedoc would certainly have some – and remove them from the pan. Add some chopped bacon and make a roux with a little flour, stir in a little white wine and stock, add some tomato purée and a boquet garni. Allow the sauce to simmer for some twelve to fifteen minutes before putting the bacon and bouquet garni in a casserole with the pigeons. Strain the sauce over the birds. Add about ten blanched cloves of garlic, cover the pan and cook for half an hour. I speak of pigeons in the plural as you will need a bird each and you would have to be strangely greedy to prepare this dish for yourself alone. Fried croutons of bread go well with this dish. Ideally the croutons too should be fried in goose fat.

I would not presume to say much about woodcock or snipe since I have never cooked either, but, as with grouse, you should take care not to overcook them. And don't imagine when you eat these little birds that you are any kinder than the cruel Italian slavering over his larks and linnets although, of course, you may find comfort in the knowledge that what you are eating was probably killed by an English gentleman.

Another little bird which comes to mind while one is on the subject of game is the quail. Although I have eaten quails and have certainly enjoyed them, I cannot claim to rate them nearly as highly as a partridge – or even a pigeon. Perhaps they are mass fattened in some odious way in tiny cages or perhaps they are just not quite as wonderful as they are commonly believed to be. Clearly I am in the minority as *Larousse Gastronomic* devotes pages to their preparation. There is no end to the time you can devote to boning them, stuffing them, wrapping them in muslin, setting them in jelly, coating them in cream, putting them in pastry and so forth.

I must admit though that quails stuffed with foie gras are tempting enough. Stuff the quails – two per person – with foie gras, brown them in butter, flamber them in brandy. Remove the quails from the pan, add a glass of white wine and allow it to boil fast for a few minutes, add some sultanas which have previously been soaked in wine, a little cream, stir and season the sauce, return the birds to the pan and, with the lid on, cook for about twelve minutes.

By October most people with gardens have a glut of apples and the shops everywhere are filled with them. How well one remembers the endless stewed apple which was thought to be suitable nursery food in the post-war years. I suppose that it was perfectly good nursery food but it did put me off apples for many years to follow. Now I have come round to them again which is just as well since my garden is filled with them at this time of year. I have already mentioned their use in connection with pheasant, pork and so forth and I have spoken in the last chapter about apple tarts and more particularly the delicious *tarte des Demoiselles Tatin*.

I still don't really like baked apples but am sure that the best ones are made from Bramleys. If you core them properly so that no little bits of "finger-nail" remain, stuff them with butter and brown sugar and slit the skin all the way round with a sharp knife they will rise like so many little soufflés in a medium to hot oven. I loathe currants with baked apples and cannot imagine why so many people add them.

A good apple purée can be made by adding some marmalade to the purée. I once had a French au pair girl who amazed me by coring and quartering, although not peeling, the apples for an apple purée. The purée was certainly excellent and the tougher parts of the skins were left behind in the food mill, but now that so many people have food mixers I imagine that the apples have to be peeled.

One of the old nursery favourites for which I do have a weakness is apple charlotte made in the following way. Butter a soufflé dish and put a layer of peeled, cored and sliced apples in the bottom and sprinkle with sugar, a pinch of cinnamon and a couple of cloves, cover the apples with slices of buttered white bread, then add more apples, more bread and butter and so on until the dish is full. Cover the dish with greased paper and bake in the oven for up to an hour.

Although I have bad memories of stewed apple, it does seem to me that with the demise of the pudding generally we have lost a lot of excellent things. Who nowadays ever serves castle puddings – those glorious little sponge puddings shaped like sand castles and sometimes tasting of ginger over which we used to pour melted golden syrup?

Once I gave a sponge pudding to a German woman who came to lunch and she exclaimed as it was brought to the table, "But, Teressa, in Chermany, ve do not eat ze hot cake!" Sad to say, we hardly ever do in England any more either, and on the rare occasions that we do I have noticed that everybody is delighted.

And so are they delighted by old-fashioned home-made chutneys

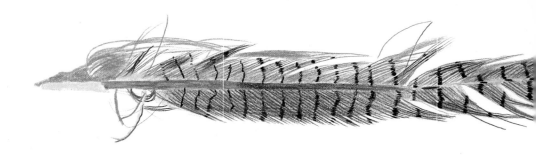

which are due to be made at this time of year. I was particularly pleased by a recipe for an uncooked chutney which I was given a few years ago.

To a pound each of dates, sultanas and onions you need a pound and a half of apples, three quarters of a pound of soft brown sugar, a pint of vinegar, two teaspoonfuls of ground ginger and two ounces of salt. The fruit and onions should be minced and mixed together, then the sugar, ginger, salt and vinegar should be added and mixed in. Leave for twenty-four hours and stir at intervals before putting the chutney into jars and covering it. The chutney is ready to eat immediately and is one of the best I know.

Another good recipe for chutney requires two pounds of green tomatoes, a pound of apples, half a pound of onions, a quarter of a pound of sultanas, an ounce of salt, half an ounce of root ginger, a tablespoonful of pickling spice and half a pound of sugar.

Tie the spice in a muslin bag, mix the chopped apples, tomatoes and onions and mix in the remainder of the ingredients except the sugar. Bring to the boil and simmer gently until the fruit is tender. Add the sugar and boil until a syrupy consistency is reached. Remove the spice bag, pour the chutney into pots and cover.

Because of the way our lives seem to have changed over the last twenty years or so and partly too because of the easy availability of foreign foods and the quantity and quality of some ready-made and frozen food, things which in the past might have seemed everyday and

unexciting, like home-made chutney and apple charlotte, have now acquired a glamour of their own with the result that people are really pleased to be offered them. Most people can't afford to eat quails stuffed with foie gras every day, nor even to serve them to their guests, and even if they could I am sure that the day would come when they would begin to long for cottage pie and green tomato chutney.

October Wines

When I was a young man it was normal to be given beer or cider at shooting lunches. Nowadays, when so many shoots are run on some sort of syndicate system which may mean that each gun has paid anything up to £400 for his day's sport, they expect something better. I am not sure it is a very good idea to drink wine at a shooting lunch, particularly as the sportsmen are usually given a glass of whisky or cherry brandy (I often cut mine with whisky as a pre-luncheon drink, to reduce the sweetness) or sometimes whisky macs – ginger wine and whisky – as they come in.

Casting my mind back over my shooting experiences in the south of England – Scotland, with its tradition of picnics, is quite different; sometimes they drink quite good wine up there out of tin mugs, a hangover from the days when they ate porridge in their fingers, walking round the table as they did so – I simply cannot remember a time when we ate anything except stews for lunch. People who shoot

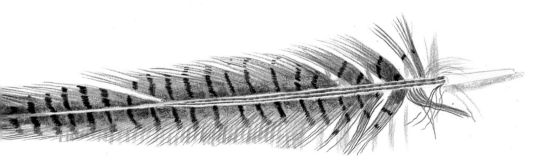

regularly four or five times a week in the season must grow fed up with
them. The wine served is nearly always an unpretentious Haut Médoc
or Bordeaux Supérieur in the 'C' range. I would not serve anything else
even if I dared. These sacred traditions are not be tampered with. The
garagistes and property developers might demand their money back.

Game pie seems an obvious thing to eat at shooting lunches, but
I cannot actually remember eating one. I have a strong theory about
jugged hare which dates from the time when my wife was so
dreadfully sick after eating one. At the time we were rather poor,
and the wine I chose to drink with it, I am sorry to say, was
Mouton Cadet, the mass-produced branded wine of the wily Baron
Philippe de Rothschild. In fact it is a perfectly safe wine, much chosen
by young men who know nothing about the subject but wish to
impress their companion without spending too much money. But,
brooding about this dreadful episode afterwards, I decided that the
wine must have been as much to blame as the jugged hare, and that it
was the combination which had caused the trouble. This led me to
experiment with various wines and the conclusion I reached was that
the only safe wine to drink with jugged hare or gamey venison was
young Syrah, best of all a fairly mild young Syrah like St. Joseph or
Crozes-Hermitage. There are some Australian Syrahs – called Shiraz –
which would do just as well, but the grander and stronger wines –
Hermitage, Côte Rotie or Cornas, often the strongest of them all when
young – might have the same effect as young claret in inflaming the
stomach and upsetting the digestive juices. One must remember that
when one talks of a dead bird – or hare, or piece of venison – as being
"high" one is talking of the natural decomposition of the flesh which
occurs after death. Beef, mutton or pork in the same condition would
be thrown away. Humans are generally buried or burned before they
can get like that. Game birds do not seem to cause trouble, possibly
because the bacteria they carry around are less harmful, possibly
because one does not eat so much of them. But one eats an enormous
amount of bad meat in a jugged hare, or in a haunch of venison, and I
am convinced that a mild bland St. Joseph or Crozes-Hermitage from
the 'C'/'D' range is the only wine to go with it.

Many of my friends groan when they see roast pheasant, but I adore
it when it comes with potato crisps, bread sauce, and always serve my
best claret or Burgundy in appreciation. Where grouse is concerned,
any but the very best and strongest claret is liable to be overshadowed,
and since no honest Englishman can now afford the clarets we used to

ESTATE BOTTLED · MISE AU CHATEAU · CHATEAUNEUF-DU-PAPE · Tête de Cru · 1979 · CHATEAU-FORTIA · PROPRIÉTÉ DU BARON LE ROY DE BOISEAUMARIÉ · CHATEAU FORTIA - 84 - CHATEAUNEUF -DU-PAPE · 75 cl · APPELLATION CHATEAUNEUF DU PAPE CONTRÔLÉE

drink twenty years ago without thinking twice about it – the Latours and the Mouton-Rothschilds – it is better to stick to medium-rank village Burgundy, which is stronger, even if it is getting hard to find under the 'G' bracket.

These wines can really be acquired only by a programme of laying down. Those who are not prepared to spend such large sums for a future consumption may be interested in another wine, which is slightly more expensive than the three mentioned for September, but which has the curious property of getting better and better almost indefinitely. Burgundies and clarets have a disagreeable way of reaching their peak and then descending, sometimes in the case of claret very abruptly. Cornas, from the northern Rhône, is a wine which tastes utterly horrible for the first four or five years of its life; thereafter it gets better and better and better for anything up to twenty-five years.

One eats woodcock so seldom that it would be a gross affectation to pretend there is any special wine to drink with them. Woodcocks' innards on toast, an even rarer dish, should be accompanied by what I call farmyard pinot, a taste sometimes found in southern Burgundies like Givry or Santenay in an "off" year like 1977. But I feel we are getting a little bit exquisite here. How many hostesses regularly serve woodcocks' (or snipes') innards on toast? Certainly not my dear wife. When I was a boy, it was a treat reserved for the lad who had shot his first woodcock (or snipe). I had it once and thought it perfectly disgusting, but had to get it down somehow as it was a special treat. I wish I had had an old burned, chaptalised Givry or Santenay, laced with young Hermitage or port, to help it down.

Quail are such a slight and subtle taste they are best served with champagne, especially if someone has kindly boned them and stuffed them with foie gras. In fact practically nobody in England eats them. I have only eaten them thus as a guest of the champagne industry in Reims, served with a wonderfully flat, maderized old vintage champagne which the French would have thrown away years ago if it were not for the strange English taste for old champagne.

It is a waste of time to drink any wine with stewed apples, especially if they have had treacle added. They should be seen more as something we have to survive in order to set a good example to those younger or less fortunate than ourselves and to avoid waste. They are a reminder of original sin, and the burden of guilt we must all carry with us for as long as we live, when greed got the better of our common ancestors. Personally, I would happily live without dessert apples if I never had to eat another stewed one. Wine is not a suitable thing to accompany these occasional acts of remorse and self-mortification.

It is a truth universally acknowledged that full fat French cheeses are at their best during the winter months. To a certain extent this is also true of dry English cheeses since in warmer weather they very quickly sweat, become greasy and acquire an acid taste.

My favourite English cheeses have always been Cheddar and Red Leicester. Everyone knows how important it is to avoid buying cheese in ready-cut slices big enough for Minnie Mouse and wrapped in plastic, but still an amazing number of grocers think they can get away with selling it like this. Of course a good grocer should allow the customer to taste the cheese before buying it.

Every year when I go to France I find that our traditional enemies have invented yet another cheese. One year it was Boursault – an excellent, creamy cheese which can now be found quite easily in England. It should be soft to the touch, but not too soft as, when over-ripe, it can taste like slightly rancid butter. Then another year I found that a goat cheese, shaped and packed like a Camembert and with the consistency of Camembert, had been launched on the French market. Again, it should be soft to the touch. But I am still faithful to the traditional type of goat cheese although this one has a good texture and a pleasant, mild taste.

With all these new cheeses just across the Channel, perhaps we should be rather ashamed of having taken a hundred years – or whatever – to produce anything so mediocre as Lymeswold, although since the appearance of Lymeswold various other new English cheeses have come on to the market. One which I particularly like is a hard goat cheese wrapped in nettles called Yarg. And some of the Somerset Brie is outstandingly good.

I have noticed that it is now becoming fashionable in really good English restaurants – and there are more and more – to have a cheese board entirely made up of English cheeses. To my mind this is a sad mistake and one which is probably based on a misplaced sense of patriotism – they will be giving us English wine next – and a probably sound sense of economy. However good Yarg or Cheddar may be, it is an absurdity for any restaurant which aims at the higher reaches of gastronomy totally to ignore the great French cheeses. And I would add that a cheese board which is made up of English cheeses only, however fine their quality, just does not begin properly to tempt as it looks drab and uninteresting and is usually accompanied by a waiter who, disregarding the finer sensitivities of the palate, produces a hard line in "buy British" sales talk.

Smart French people will endlessly disscuss the rights and wrongs of eating butter with cheese. The only real guide-lines seems to be whether or not you come from Normandy. The greedy Normans naturally put butter and cream with everything. It seems to me that if you like your Camembert to be ripe – without the faintest chalky streak in the centre – then you won't really need butter. But it is quite wrong to suppose that all French people like their Camemberts to be very strong and runny. There are many who prefer them before they are *à point*. When choosing a Camembert one should not just prod the top of the cheese which may have been damaged by many other prodding fingers, but it should be taken out of the box and the underneath of the cheese gently pressed. It is also essential to smell a Camembert before buying it as, if it has no smell, it will have no taste.

The best Camemberts, and the only ones which I will buy, are made from unpasteurised milk. The box will always tell you whether or not the milk has been pasteurised.

A particularly elegant way of serving a ripe Camembert – I have only ever seen this done in Paris – is to scrape the crust with a serrated knife so as to make the outside of the cheese sticky, and then to roll it in finely pounded digestive biscuits. My French friends must, I think, have used Petit béurre biscuits.

I think a good cheese board should have at least one, ripe, classic cheese, I do not believe that anything can ever beat a well chosen Camembert, although a Reblochon or a Pont l'Eveque may run a close second. Both these can go over the top very quickly, but at the same time they smell so strong that when they are at their best they already smell vile. If, like all these restaurateurs and waiters, you are especially patriotic, a large chunk of your favourite English cheese – Cheshire or Wensleydale or whatever – will contrast nicely with the French cheese.

The cheese counters in many English grocers' shops are filled these days with some particularly repulsive-looking pink and green mottled stuff which reminds me of nothing so much as a baby's thighs. I cannot imagine who buys it although a great many people must do so judging by the amount of it around.

It is a funny thing that a fat French cheese which has been started the day before and which is just beginning to spread across the cheese board is most inviting, partly because people can judge its degree of ripeness, whereas a piece of half-eaten Cheddar has no appeal at all.

It is quite difficult to buy a creamy goat cheese in England. They really should be allowed to ripen in a warm room before being added to your cheese board. Perhaps the reason why a lot of people do not seem to like goat cheese is because it is often too dry and powdery – which in fact means that it is under-ripe.

As far as blue cheeses are concerned – and no cheese board is complete without one – I used to think that I would go for the Italian Gorgonzola, or the rather milder Dolce Latte which is, in fact, a type of processed Gorgonzola. In fact I was once greatly mocked by some Italians for daring to say that I liked Dolce Latte which they said was not even a cheese.

More recently I have been won round to the glories of Roquefort which, if taken seriously, is one of the most interesting cheeses available and one which varies in quality and taste quite as much as any other. In fact, unlike Camembert, Reblochon and so forth, the best season for Roquefort is not the winter, but the summer. All the same, I should say that this cheese can be eaten with impunity all the year round.

Real Roquefort originates from a little town in the Aveyron called Roquefort-sur-Soulzon where it is made from the curds of ewes' milk and dried breadcrumbs. These crumbs, when dried, are ground to a fine powder and then allowed to develop a mould. The cheeses are left to ripen in the cool, damp, calcareous caves of the region. A good Roquefort should be creamy, yellowish in colour and evenly veined. Much of the Roquefort on sale is factory-produced these days but a good French cheese merchant will allow you to taste his different Roqueforts and once you have tasted the real thing you will never forget it nor be taken in by an inferior one again.

My younger son at the age of about fifteen deeply impressed a stall holder in a French market town by tasting all the Roqueforts and instantly picking out the best and most expensive one which had been made traditionally and ripened in the chalky caves of the Causses. I earned a lot of kudos that morning and have since been treated with great respect by that particular cheesemonger all because of *le petit* who can really recognize a good Roquefort.

Cream cheeses such as Boursin are all right, but only just. I have a feeling that Boursin, like Caprice des Dieux, may have deteriorated over the years in any case, both of them have a vaguely plastic,

chemical taste to me. But there are a thousand different excellent
French cheeses to choose from – Saint-Albray, Chaume, Tomme de
Savoie, Munster, Vacherin, which is eaten in France with a spoon at
Christmas time, not to mention Emmenthal and Gruyère which are of
course Swiss, although the French are happy to forget that fact.

I have discovered that dry Dutch Edam is a good cheese with which
to cook – better than Cheddar, less gooey than Gruyère and quite
tasty. It is certainly better than powdered Parmesan sold in little
cardboard boxes. In fact some French cheesemongers allow whole
Edam cheeses to dry and then sell them specifically for cooking.

When it comes to cooking, it is of course true that for some dishes
you can actually need the gooey consistency of Gruyère or
Emmenthal, as for instance in *suprêmes au fromage*. Beat three eggs in
a bowl, season and little by little add half a litre of boiling milk,
beating all the time. Add some grated Gruyère and mix well. Butter
some ramekins, pour in the mixture and cook in an oven in a bain-
marie for fifteen minutes. Turn out the *supremes* and serve with a
cheese sauce, a tomato sauce, or perhaps a béchamel sauce to which
you have added some grated cheese and puréed spinach.

For a cheese soufflé, contrary to all instructions, I use self-raising
flour and a mixture of Emmenthal or Gruyère and Parmesan and at
least five whites of egg. Famous last words: I have never failed yet
which is strange as until I had a Magimix food processor I was totally
incapable of making a cake which rose.

If like me you have a son – or friend for that matter, – who is totally
obsessed by Roquefort, you could make toasted cheese by spreading
slices of bread with a mixture made from a thick béchamel, melted
Roquefort, an egg and a little mustard. Toast one side of the bread
before turning it, spreading on the cheese mixture and grill for a few
minutes.

Perhaps most people don't associate cheese with winter time quite
in the way that I do, but there can be no doubt about it that when it
comes to something like a cassoulet, then that is undoubtedly a dish
for a cold November day.

For over twenty years now I have been a regular visitor to
Castelnaudary in south-west France. The region is little known to
tourists although crowds of hispanophiles hurtle through to Barcelona
without a sideways glance, and a few languid travellers sit munching
saucisson on barges as they sail down the Canal du Midi from
Bordeaux to Sète.

Those entering Castelnaudary by road will be greeted by a sign which reads: "CASTELNAUDARY, *son moulin, son port de plaisance, sa piscine olympique, son Cassoulet.*" "*Ses alléluias* " and "*glorias*", which are rather indifferent biscuits, still exist but are no longer advertised as tempting fare for the passing traveller.

Castelnaudary is in the Aude. It lies beneath the foothills of the Massif Central, in the Plaine du Lauragais which, in its turn, stretches across to the foothills of the Pyrenees. In mediaeval times the Aude was ravaged by religious wars. The ruins of many fine Cathar castles like Montségur, Peyrepertuse and Quéribus bear witness to this past, but the Cassoulet de Castelnaudary still reigns supreme in the present, and Chauriens, as the natives of Castelnaudary are called, argue perpetually about the correct way to make it.

Many legends are told concerning the origin of Cassoulet. One such claims that when Castlenaudary was besieged during the religious wars every inhabitant brought his all and threw it into one steaming pot – a bean, a sausage, a tomato – but the respect I bear the French forbids me to believe such tales.

The French, as we all know, are extremely good at cooking, they are also very economical and each region has its own speciality made from the most easily available ingredients.

Here, in the Aude, the most easily available ingredients were pork, beans and goose. The Chauriens, however, claim that goose should not be included in a cassoulet – but only pork. Goose, they say, is a perversion introduced by the people of Toulouse.

When I first came to the Aude I made friends with a wonderful old lady, said to be a white witch, who made the best cassoulet in the region. People came from all over the neighbourhood, bringing their ingredients, their special Cassoulet dish – a round, open, earthernware one – and for a few francs she would do the work. This splendid lady taught me how to make cassoulet (without goose), she also crocheted a fine bedspread for me, but, sadly, she is now crippled by arthritis and we must all learn to fend for ourselves.

Apart from the goose versus pork argument, which I will deal with later, there is an argument which says that cassoulet cannot be made anywhere but in the area around Castelnaudary. The mere suggestion of making Cassoulet in Paris is so outrageous that it can hardly be any worse to make it in England.

In my experience everything tastes different, not necessarily accord-

ing to the recipe only, but according to the cook, the climate, the water and so forth, and there is therefore nothing absurd about attempting to make a cassoulet de Castelnaudary in the United Kingdom or in the United States. It makes an excellent dish for a cold winter's day and some of our American friends might even consider substituting it for their traditional Thanksgiving turkey.

Here, anyway, is my friend's recipe. Take a pound of white haricot beans and put them to soak overnight. The proper sausages to use are *saucisses de Toulouse* and these may be hard to come by: The nearest thing to a *saucisse de Toulouse* is a pure pork sausage with no additive whatsoever except pepper. If you cannot find an honest sausage, you cannot make do with the beige rubbish which generally calls itself a sausage in England, but go to an Italian grocer and buy Italian sausages. (I hear the Chauriens scream in horror.) If you have never been to Castelnaudary, or if you have an open mind, you will be perfectly happy. So, take a pound of beans, a sausage, or piece of sausage per person, a pound of loin of pork cut into chunks and a few pieces of pig skin, known in France as *couenne*. Boil the soaked beans for about an hour and keep the liquid they have cooked in on one side. Melt a large onion in fat and brown all the meats. Into the cassoulet dish put alternate layers of beans and meat and onion, season each layer, add two cloves of garlic, a good sprig of thyme, two chopped, peeled tomatoes, a tablespoonful of tomato purée. Fill the dish up with the liquid from the beans. If there is not enough, add water. The cassoulet should then be cooked slowly in the oven for a good three hours. It should not be served immediately, but left until the next day and reheated with the addition of more water, if necessary. A good cassoulet should be neither stodgy, nor too runny and the top should be covered with a thick crunchy crust. No accompaniment is necessary, but a green salad to follow is ideal.

Now, as far as goose is concerned I hate to betray my hosts and friends of twenty years, but I am forced to admit that goose is a delicious addition to a cassoulet. Goose and pork may be used together – the sausage and *couenne* are never omitted – or goose may be used on its own. The goose in question is tinned, preserved in its own fat and very expensive. The goosefat is used to brown the meats. Otherwise the cassoulet is made in the same way as I have described.

Cassoulet may not quite rate with bouillabaisse but I prefer it to choucroûte and it certainly deserves a wider public than it has – provided it is made with care.

With the approach of winter a greedy fellow's thoughts naturally turn not only to cassoulet but to all sorts of stews and suchlike warming dishes. It is a shame that the very word "stew" conjures up, for many people, the unforgettable picture of school dinners – thick greasy gravy and lumps of fatty, sinewy meat. My own dear husband, a man not given to refusing food, was beaten at his prep school for hurling gristly, fatty stew under the table. Unfortunately a lump settled on the knee of Mr Trapps Lomax, the Mathematics master who always wore shorts. Perhaps it is this sort of association which has caused the odious euphemism "casserole" to creep into the English language. As every educated person knows, the French word *casserole* means saucepan. Fewer people are likely to know that it also means a tinny piano. What it does not mean is a stew.

In any case there is no reason why a stew should be either fatty or greasy. It is perfectly easy to trim your meat carefully before cooking it. Melt the onions, garlic and a chopped carrot in good-quality fat before browning the meat. Then flamber it with brandy or marc or even whisky. Never, never, never use stale left-over dregs of second-rate wine to cook your stew, but rather a good glass of freshly opened Rhône red. Let the wine bubble before adding stock to cover the meat, more carrots and herbs. A turnip not only adds flavour to a stew, but helps to thicken the gravy. A little tomato purée also helps to thicken the gravy. Cook your stew slowly for a long time and serve it with boiled potatoes. In my opinion mashed potatoes are unacceptable with stews. Besides the potatoes you only need to serve a green salad afterwards. Crowded, messy plates are quite unappealing.

If you don't really fancy a stew, *pot au feu* is an excellent dish often served at large family meals in France. For this you need a pan big enough to hold a piece of beef (either brisket or silverside), and vegetables. Use a variety of vegetables including onions, carrots, turnips, celery and leeks. A clove or two of garlic will not go amiss and you should add a good bouquet garni. Bring the beef to the boil first, with some of the vegetables, and cook slowly for about two hours before adding the rest of the vegetables. None of the vegetables should be finely sliced and the onions should be left whole. Continue cooking for another hour or so.

This is a remarkably good and practical dish which provides you with an excellent soup as a first course. Serve the meat with either a tomato sauce or a vinaigrette made with French mustard and to which you have added chopped whites of hard-boiled egg and a generous amount of chopped mixed herbs.

For those people who are not tempted by large pieces of meat, why not try stuffing a cabbage. There are various ways of doing this. If you are using a white cabbage, blanch it and separate the leaves. Wrap the stuffing in individual leaves and bake in a flat dish with a little stock for about an hour. But, if you are using a green cabbage, blanch it, open the cabbage out and remove the heart. For the stuffing, melt a chopped onion and brown some minced pork, add the chopped heart of the

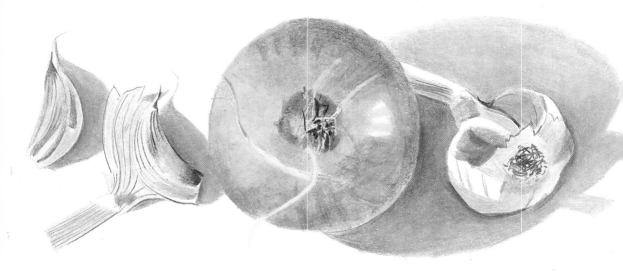

cabbage, herbs, seasoning, a couple of chopped peeled tomatoes, garlic, a tablespoonful of red wine and a cupful of blanched rice. Fill the outer leaves of the cabbage with the stuffing and tie into shape. Place the cabbage in a deep, earthenware dish, add stock to halfway up the cabbage, cover the dish and cook in the oven for about two hours.

Of course not only does every part of France have its own traditional country fare like Cassoulet or *coq berrichon* or *boeuf à la bourguignonne*, but there are *estouffades, carbonnades*, goulashes and ox-tail stews to be considered, not to mention Irish Stew and *blanquette de veau*.

For a *boeuf à la bourguignonne*, dice the beef, brown it gently in dripping or oil, add some small whole onions and when they are browned add a dessertspoonful of flour, stir until the flour has browned a little, add a crushed clove of garlic and wine and water to cover the meat. Add a little tomato purée, salt, pepper and a bouquet garni, cover the pan and cook slowly for about three and a half hours. Add the mushrooms a quarter of an hour before serving.

A *carbonnade* is one of my favourite ways of stewing beef. For this you can use shin of beef or, better still, chuck. The beef should be cut into large slices and browned. Slice and brown several onions. Put a layer of onions in the bottom of a pan and then the meat, season and add a second layer of onions. Season again, add a bouquet garni, cover with some good strong beer or Guinness, and a slice of bread thickly spread with mustard on both sides, cover the pan and cook slowly, preferably in the oven, for about four hours. This like most stews is better when heated up, which also means that you can remove the fat from the sauce when it is cold. Serve with boiled potatoes or rice.

For a *daube* you should lard each piece of diced beef with a strip of bacon rolled in parsley and chopped garlic. Place the meat in a pan on a layer of pork rind or streaky bacon, add the sliced onions and carrots, seasoning and boquet garni, cover with red wine and cook slowly for about four hours. Thicken the sauce with a couple of dessertspoonfuls of tomato purée. ,

When one comes to think of it, one could eat a different stew almost every day of the month. By the time one had done that throughout November and had, too, one's fair share of Camembert and Reblochon, one would hardly want to bother about Christmas.

November Wines

Cheese and different types of stew seem to make up the diet for November. Better than jam and jellied eels, I suppose. Despite having been married for twenty-five years to a lady whose stews are like fairy food, I find I still feel queasy at any mention of the word. Surely the worst stews ever put before human beings were made at All Hallows, Cranmore, Shepton Mallet, Somerset thirty-five years ago, although they were closely followed in horror by those served at Downside and the Guards Depot, Caterham five and ten years later. Even now my throat closes to think of them. That is why I am not shocked to hear them called "casseroles". You could call them bath tubs or fire engines for all I care. Anything to avoid the word "stew". I remember I stopped reading *Wind in the Willows* when I was ten at the point where Mr Toad finds a gypsy eating a delicious stew. I realized then the book was meant for grown-ups.

The best wine to drink with really disgusting food, in my experience, is an old Syrah from St Joseph, in the northern Rhône. There is something comforting, emollient, anodyne, even medicinal about a 1976 St Joseph Le Grand Pompée from Jaboulet. All the acid it ever had has disappeared, leaving a bland, herbal taste which seems to line the stomach and protect it. Much healthier than eating Kaolin, which is what was recommended to people drinking home-distilled hooch during Prohibition, and was said to line their stomachs with the most delicate porcelain.

But that is by the way. There is no danger that any of my wife's delicious suggestions will call for such treatment. It used to be said that where you use wine for cooking you should always drink the same or similar wine with the eating – thus, with *poule au Chambertin* you drank Chambertin, with *boeuf bourguignonne* you drank whatever Burgundy. I do not know whether there is wisdom in this convention, or whether it is just superstition, but where you are flavouring your stew with a glass of freshly opened Rhône red, as she suggests, it seems more likely than not that you will be drinking a freshly opened Rhone red with your meal. Perhaps it will turn out to be the 1976 St Joseph Le Grande Pompée. More likely, I should have thought, some humble Côtes du Rhone generic, which is really quite good enough for stews.

Time and again, reading through the proposed meals for November (a different stew *every* day?), I found myself murmuring: "Something red, and rich, and deep." The truth is that to my taste *all* the best reds are rich and concentrated and deep, but one really does not want to drink an expensive classic Burgundy or Bordeaux or even one of the best Hermitages or Côtes Rôties with a stew – unless, that is, one happens to be rich enough to drink these marvellous wines every day.

Even then, I feel, one might die of over-indulgence, as one is said to do
if one eats pigeon every day for a month. If one pursues the argument
of drinking the wine used in cooking, I suppose one should drink beer
with the *carbonnade*. Quite possibly the Flemings do, but there is no
reason why we should copy Belgians in their gross, uncouth habits.

When I was a boy, it was quite normal for country houses to serve
beer or cider for luncheon, wine only in the evening. Indeed, I suspect
it was considered *nouveau riche*, or somehow ungentlemanly, to drink
wine at luncheon. My father, who adopted many of the customs and
attitudes of the upper class, never adopted this one, thank God, and we
always had wine, but my mother's family, of nobler lineage, never
served anything but beer or cider for luncheon in the country, at any
rate until comparatively recently. There are still country houses which
stick to this convention, but I suspect they are being self-consciously
vieille Angleterre and that it is an affectation. The truth, as I see it, is
that beer is not something to be drunk with meals, unless in prison on
Christmas Day, except very occasionally in the summer with cold food
of a particularly gross variety – pork pie and Cheddar cheese, ham
salad, etc. In fact, with pub food. Never with cold salmon or any of
summer's real delights.

Cider is slightly different. In Somerset it is sometimes served, rather
self-consciously, as the *vin de pays*, but only by the poor or the mean.
For the poor, of course, one should always feel bottomless com-
passion, even in November. I never serve it myself, but sometimes
drink it when I am particularly anxious to stay sober – usually when I
have an enormous amount of work to do in the afternoon. It is not a
very nasty drink, but it is not a very nice one, either. As a Somerset
man, I would like to recommend a particular producer from my own
region, but I am ashamed to say that the best I have found comes from
Kent and Sussex, in the sweeter Merrydown "vintage" label. Somerset
farmhouse cider is and always has been, utterly disgusting. In recent
years there has been a cult of dry cider – possibly in response to the
fashion for dry things inspired by the late Ian Fleming which reached
its final reduction to absurdity in the almost completely tasteless
"extra brut" champagnes. In my view, cider's greatest weakness is its
shortage of taste; to receive the fullest taste of apples, it is essential to
choose a sweet cider – in fact, the sweeter the better. The idea that it is
somehow more sophisticated to serve a dry cider seems to me utterly
wrong. Cider is not a sophisticated taste, and it is a waste of time to
pretend the contrary. It is essentially a low taste, and I prefer it fizzy.

But one forgives the serving even of dry cider with luncheon more readily than the serving of home-made wines. By "home-made wines" I am not referring to the products of the growing English wine industry, whose devotees labour night and day to produce something drinkable from various hybrid combinations of the Riesling and Sylvaner grape, usually under the most appalling climatic conditions. English wine for all the love and care which goes into it is bad enough. I have certainly never tasted one which was better than drinkable, usually with a boiled-sweet taste of the sort which winemakers in the Touraine have recently learned to extract from the Colombard grape. The cost of production is so high that English wines will never be able to compete with those from better favoured regions. But the chief horror of English hospitality is the home-made wine, sometimes made from elderberry or apple, but more often from parsnip, potato, blackberry, dandelion and a host of improbable vegetables. They are chiefly made by the wives of retired bank managers from the Midlands, settled with their budgerigars in new bungalows for them in the centre of an old village (this sacred process known by the code-name of "in-filling" has deep mystical significance in country life) and anxious to acquaint themselves with country ways.

It is not just that these "wines" are particularly horrible to drink. They are popularly endowed with quasi-miraculous alcoholic powers, but in truth they are fairly low-strength causing diarrhoea and lower-motor failure through the presence of some poison or other. Mercifully, they are usually served in minute glasses, and never with meals. One is supposed to joke about being drunk as one drinks them.

I have only once drunk a serious wine with cassoulet – it was a Beychevelle '62 – and did not feel that the wine was well served . In the Aude, we invariably eat it with the best of the local wines, a Fitou from one corner of the huge Corbières wine-producing area. It is not a particularly magnificent wine, but anything better would be wasted, and various Fitous are widely available in Britain nowadays, notably a Cuvée Madame Parmentier from Oddbin in the 'B' price range. Although cheap, it improves with a year or two in bottle, which means that one should always go for the oldest wine on offer. It is certainly not worth storage space in one's own cellar.

As soon as I hear that tomato purée has been added to a stew – or tomatoes in any form, for that matter – I find myself reaching for Italian wines. This may seem superstitious, but the Italians eat tomatoes with practically everything. I do not believe that the sharp taste of tomatoes – and they *should* taste sharp – improves any wine very much; Italian wines are used to coping with it. The best Italian wine I have yet discovered (apart from a few high-priced prestige labels like Tignanello) comes from Barolo, made by Poderi Maccarini, and called La Brunate. This is seriously good wine, its rich, thick, malty taste well enough cut with acid to cope with any amount of tomatoes. Unfortunately, it is priced just within the 'E' range from Recount Wines and many people at the time of writing are simply not prepared to spend over £5.50 on an Italian wine. One can perfectly well drink a Chianti Putto in the 'B' range, but some of those wines from Barolo are really excellent.

I have already expounded my views on the great wine-and-cheese debate. Since they fly in the teeth of all expert opinion – including such great men as Hugh Johnson, who knows a hundred times as much about wine as I do – I will merely repeat them. It is the act of a madman to drink Burgundy or any other table wine with ripe Camembert, Reblochon, Pont l'Evêque or any other strong, soft cheese. These cheeses not only drown the taste of the wine, but set up some chemical reaction and makes it taste of ammonia and tin. The best thing to drink with these cheeses is tawny port – preferably an old one. My favourites, in mounting order of cost, are Cockburn's Ten Year Old, Harvey's Directors' Bin, Taylor's Twenty Year Old. Even the best vintage ports can be thrown out by these strong cheeses, although they cope very well with Stilton and all milder cheeses. Where mild cheeses like New Zealand Cheddar and Caerphilly are concerned, it doesn't really matter what you drink, since every wine ever made goes admirably well with them.

Where cooked cheese is concerned – especially anything with Gruyère or Emmenthal in it – I usually like a thickish red or opulent white with that slightly mean taste of mouse-droppings which one finds chiefly in farmyard Syrah – either Cornas or Crozes-Hermitage – and in Alsatian Gewürztraminer, preferably a *vendage tardive*. These last are usually quite expensive and hard to find, but the miraculous year 1983 produced a large quantity which should be around for several years, at present in the 'D' range but likely to climb. Where cooked Stilton and Roquefort are concerned, my advice would be: don't cook them.

DECEMBER

With the advent of December come all the more odious trappings of Christmas – the smudgy reproductions of paintings by the elder Breughel, the crowded shops full of overpriced junk, the fairy-lights, the tinsel, the pressure to be gay (in the pristine sense of the word), the Regent Street lights, the canned carols in the shopping precincts, the poinsettias, the pictures of robins, of snowmen, of hansom cabs and so on for ever. As Sir Lawrence Jones once wrote:

> A pert young angel plucked the Master's dress
> 'This picture of a snowman comes from earth
> It celebrates a certain person's birth.
> Guess Lord whose.' The Master couldn't guess.

Well, it happens every year and every year most of us sigh and groan and wonder how we are going to pay for it all or if we will ever be ready on time for the great day, and yet, when the great day finally comes, we usually enjoy ourselves. I think that perhaps one of the best moments during the whole of Christmas is that moment on Christmas Eve when you realize that the shops have at last shut. There is nothing left to do but to have a good time. If you have no brandy for the brandy butter or if you have forgotten to buy a present for your husband or wife – well, then it is too late – so what the hell?

One year we had the wonderful idea of spending Christmas in the Danieli Hotel in Venice. It was not so wildly extravagant as it may sound since such hotels offer package prices in the winter. Nevertheless the whole experience was one of amazing luxury. It was a week of complete escapism and escapism is perhaps the greatest of all luxuries.

But if you cannot afford to spend Christmas in the old-fashioned luxury of the Danieli, you may still feel that something a little different from the over-familiar Brussels sprout might be welcome. We ate not one Brussels sprout during our week in Venice.

Some people thrive on tradition – others may be appalled by its ties, or even by the thought of doing the same thing at the same time on the same day as everyone else in England.

A goose, as the Yorkshire yeoman said, is a silly bird – not enough for two and too much for one. It is certainly the case that a goose will not go very far in a large family, which is a shame as it is a much more interesting bird than a turkey. It can be stuffed for roasting with an excellent mixture of chopped and fried bacon, onions and apple to which are added chopped walnuts and celery leaves, some thyme, a clove of garlic, salt, pepper, a handful of breadcrumbs and an egg to bind. It is necessary when cooking goose – or indeed a duck – to be careful to drain all the fat off before making the gravy. Indeed it is a good idea to remove some of the fat halfway through the cooking.

Anyone preferring to break entirely with tradition may consider buying a *zampone* from one of the Italian shops in Soho. A *zampone* is a pig's trotter stuffed with the same pork mixture as is used to make

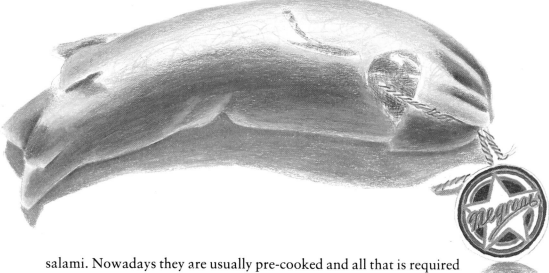

salami. Nowadays they are usually pre-cooked and all that is required is to boil them slowly for about half an hour to heat them through. *Zamponi* are often eaten at Christmas or New Year in Italy and are served with an accompaniment of lentils or haricot beans.

Haricot beans, incidentally, also make an excellent winter salad. The dressing should be added to them while they are still hot. Some chopped garlic should be mixed in. Chopped, crisply grilled streaky bacon can be another good addition.

A duck terrine is quite a trouble to make and for this reason one does not do so often, but I usually make one at Christmas and it is rich and delicious and very suitable for festive occasions.

Other cold meats may include a fresh tongue. It is, as I have said, quite difficult to find a butcher who does not automatically salt his tongues. Salted tongue can be good but I prefer it fresh, in any case it is important to know what the butcher is selling you.

Simmer the tongue slowly for about three hours with the usual onion, garlic, herbs, carrot, turnip if you have one, and a stick of celery. Keep the liquid you have cooked it in. No stock is more delicious than the broth from a tongue. While the tongue is still hot skin it. It is both easy and fun to skin. When the tongue is cold slice it as thinly as possible and dress it with an oil and vinegar dressing to which you have added a handful of chopped parsley, a chopped shallot and some thyme. If you prefer the tongue hot, it is delicious with boiled potatoes and a good, thick tomato sauce.

When in France I ate a *tête de veau* in sorrel sauce I was very keen to come home and make such a dish in England. But, as I have said, it is not easy to find a calf's head in England so I decided that the thing to do was to make my sorrel sauce and serve it with fresh tongue – then of course came the ridiculous moment of truth. Not only could I not find a calf's head, but I had no sorrel. In fact it is almost impossible to find sorrel in England unless you grow it in your garden or are prepared to tramp the fields looking for the wild variety. Desperate for a new sauce for my tongue which I had by this time acquired, I decided to make a spinach sauce along the lines of the extremely simple sorrel sauce the secrets of which had been divulged to us by a generous chef.

Reduce some of the stock in which the tongue has cooked and in it cook some spinach and a peeled and sliced cooking apple. When the spinach is well cooked put the mixture in a blender, then return the sauce to the pan, adjust the seasoning, add a squeeze of lemon juice and stir in a pot of thick cream and a teaspoonful of Dijon mustard. Pour the sauce over the sliced tongue.

The original sorrel recipe did not include an apple, but it seemed to me that, with spinach as a substitute for sorrel, some little extra tartness was required.

I find it hard to believe that everyone does not know how to cook a whole smoked ham or gammon. But as I have frequently been asked how I do it, perhaps I should mention it here. Put it in a large pan with two quarts of sweet cider and water to cover. Cook it slowly for twenty minutes to the pound and twenty minutes extra. It is difficult to over-cook a ham but, if you do, it will become crumbly. When the ham is cooked skin it, put it on a baking dish, stick as many cloves as you possibly can into the fat and then pat a thick layer of soft, dark brown sugar over the top. Put the ham into a hot oven and leave it there until the sugar has slightly caramelized – about ten minutes.

Carving is certainly an art. I have never known anyone carve so skilfully as my mother. No electric carving knife can replace her. Very thin slices should be carved – they are not only more economical but they undoubtedly taste better. If you know anyone like my mother, allow that person – and no one else – to touch your ham.

A little champagne poured straight on your plate, over your thinly carved slices of ham, is an unwonted delight.

Christmas pudding can be wonderful but which of us would really want it without the brandy butter? Most households invest in a Christmas Stilton – to my mind one of the most over-rated cheeses in the world and an excuse for drinking more port. Why not have a change, avoid the "scoop" or "slice" argument and buy a very large, whole goat cheese? All the eating and drinking at Christmas make puddings seem quite superfluous. When excellent tangerines or clementines are so easily available, why leave mince pies to moulder in the larder?

One of the glories of my childhood which might perhaps be revived is a "snapdragon". Currants, sultanas, a mixture of nuts and some sixpenny pieces were all put on a flat dish. Brandy was then poured over the dish and lighted. The brave dipped their hands in to see what they could retrieve. The cowardly wept. Nowadays, of course, there would have to be 50p. or pound coins which may be easier to pick up, but they are not nearly so pretty as sixpences.

Fortunately Christmas comes but once a year. If it came more often we would surely have to do something about it. Even the most enthusiastic devotees of Christmas could hardly bear to go through the whole thing again in June. Really, a biennial Christmas would probably suit us all better – or what a good idea it would be if Christmas and Leap Year could swap places.

Be that as it may, Christmas is with us again and the best thing to do when confronted by the absurd is, according to the French writer Albert Camus, to revolt. And how are we to revolt? By refusing to despair. So we must throw ourselves, heart and soul, into Christmas and make sure we enjoy every moment of it, whatever our reservations.

My own mother who carves so beautifully has decided on a personal form of revolt in recent years. And an excellent idea it is too. She makes chicken liver pâtés and gives them to her friends and relations instead of baubles and bangles fought for in the overcrowded shops. Anyone receiving one of these pâtés is a truly lucky person since my mother is a truly good cook. But there is no reason why other enlightened persons should not follow her lead.

There is no doubt in my mind that a well-made, home-made pâté or terrine is infinitely preferable to a tinned one from any part of France. Do not confuse *foie gras en bloc* with pâté de foie gras. It is not the same thing since it has had *nothing* added to it, but is a whole, unadulterated, goose or duck liver and as such is infinitely better.

When making a pâté or a terrine yourself it is important to remember to add enough port and brandy. I think that the lack of alcohol is what makes many of the pâtés on the market so insipid. Elizabeth David's recipe for duck terrine in her *Summer Cooking* is the one which I always use. There is nothing to beat it and I shall continue to recommend it for as long as I have an appetite. A pheasant terrine could of course be made using the same recipe.

If, on the other hand, you prefer the idea of sweetmeats, you might like to try your hand at truffles or home-made chocolates. For the latter you will need some paper cases. Line the cases with melted dark chocolate and allow the chocolate to set before putting in your filling which could be a ball of marzipan, a piece of crystallized ginger or anything else which takes your fancy. Cover the filling with more melted chocolate and leave to set.

For truffles, which can be unutterably delicious, melt the dark chocolate with a little milk, add just under half the quantity of butter, and mix in – off the heat – the yolk of an egg. Leave for a few hours before shaping into small balls and rolling in cocoa.

There is no doubt that home-made fudge is another welcome present. I have never met anyone who could resist fudge and Mrs

Beeton provides a simple recipe for it. In fact Mrs Beeton gives us as many as twelve pages of recipes for sweets many of which, I am afraid to say, are not very tempting. I was wondering, as I perused her pages, whether I could find out how to make the huge slabs of nutty toffee which are for sale all over Italy at Christmas time. But then I thought that that would be just the sort of sticky mess destined to be found glued to the back of the larder a year later.

If you prefer to make biscuits, both flapjacks and shortbread are easy to make and good to eat. I do not have a particularly sweet tooth, but if anyone wants to give me some truffles or some flapjacks, I will be extremley grateful. Neither would I say no to a brandy snap or two.

A chocolate biscuit cake is another wonderful thing, made with equal quantities of cocoa, sugar and butter, twice the quantity of pounded rich tea biscuits and an egg. Beat the butter and sugar together, add the egg, pounded biscuits and cocoa. Flatten the mixture on a tin, coat with melted dark chocolate, slice into fingers when cool and leave to harden in the refrigerator overnight.

Perhaps you should have thought back in the summer of putting peaches or pears into brandy. The peaches should be dipped in boiling water, skinned and halved and the pears (preferably dry ones) should be poached, peeled and halved before being placed in layers in air-tight jars. A little sugar should be sprinkled over each layer of fruit and the jar filled up with brandy.

If on the other hand you wish to buy a really good eating present, foie gras is clearly the thing to go for. Pâté de foie gras is a luxury indeed, a delight whose praises most Englishmen are loud in singing whilst they remain totally ignorant of the true glory of Perigord and the Languedoc.

In the Languedoc they sneer at pâté de foie gras, saying that it is a money-making scheme invented by Alsatians. For my part, I have never appreciated the little black truffles you find in it and I wonder how many people believe in all honesty that those little truffles enrich their lives. Whatever the case, pâté de foie gras, although delicious, is a mere shadow – a pale echo – of the *foie* from which it is derived and which can be bought in its original form as *foie d'oie entier en bloc*. It is worth knowing that duck liver *en bloc* is arguably as good as goose liver and slightly cheaper.

We have all heard how those cruel *parlez-vous* across the Channel force-feed their geese through funnels, and most of us, being escapists, choose not to dwell on the matter, but the devoted gourmet will tell you that the geese love to be thus gorged. Indeed they cannot get enough of it. However it may be, the result is a huge liver which wise Frenchmen and Frenchwomen put untreated into tins with nothing but a little salt.

These geese are killed in November – I have two French friends who hurry south from the Belgian border at this time of year so that they can choose the livers in the market and tin them themselves. It appears that three-quarters of the art lies in knowing how to pick a good liver.

Should you be lucky enough to be given a *bloc de foie entier* for Christmas, be careful what you do with it.

First of all, keep it in the fridge. Secondly, when you open the tin, do not remove the fat which surrounds the liver. It is delicious. Some livers have rather a lot of fat and goose livers usually have more than duck livers. Whatever you do, do not throw it away. If you can't bear to eat it as it is, use it in cooking.

Using a knife dipped in hot water to prevent the *foie* from sticking to it, cut the liver into thin slices and arrange them on a dish which you should leave in the fridge until you are ready to sit down.

The liver can be eaten as a first course or it can be eaten, as it often is in the Languedoc, after the main course and with the salad. Surprisingly enough, there is nothing more delicious than Sauternes to drink with a good foie, although some people may prefer Champagne.

There is a dreadful tendency among the English to put any decent charcuterie on thickly buttered bread. More refined persons are disgusted when they see this happening. Foie gras is far too exquisite to be treated as a mere sandwich spread. Forget about nursery teas for the moment, take a fork and savour the glorious *foie* as it deserves to be savoured for there is nothing to beat the delicate flavour and the subtlety of a first-rate liver.

Of course one cannot expect to do nothing but exchange tins of foie gras on Christmas Day and there are plenty of other delicacies to be considered. What can one give which will not be found still lurking in the back of the larder by the end of August?

I would like a Guinness fruit cake in a tin or a huge jar of ginger. Ginger is delicious served with really thick cream. I'm not sure how much mustard I want. A great deal of mustard has changed hands at Christmas but I believe that there is nothing better than good, old-fashioned English mustard or Grey Poupon. Dijon mustard is certainly better than English mustard in salad dressing and sauces. I would be grateful for a tin of Greek olive oil. Olive oil is now expensive enough to qualify as a present. I would quite like a *panetone* – available at most Italian shops. These huge cakes are far more exciting than they look and are wonderful eaten with stewed or bottled fruit. As most people have a ham at Christmas, there must be a place on every table for the brandied peach. Brandied peaches are a rare treat and in my experience they only turn up at Christmas time.

It is impossible to shy away completely from the subject of turkey at Christmas time. I have spoken elsewhere of the delicious stuffing which is to be made with the turkey livers. Apart from that, I rather like one which is made from apple and celery which Mrs Beeton recommends for use with goose or pork, but which I have frequently and successfully used with turkey.

Brown some diced pork or sausage meat in dripping. Remove the pork and cook the chopped onion and celery in the same fat for about five minutes. Remove the onions and celery and cook the chopped apples. Mix the ingredients with some breadcrumbs and chopped parsley and season. Chopped walnuts are good added to this stuffing.

But the true secret of turkey, as everyone knows, is that it is not just the stuffing that counts, but the stuffing, the sausage meat, the bacon, the bread sauce, the chipolatas, the gravy, the roast potatoes, the Brussels sprouts – in fact the whole production.

Just remember, as you carve your turkey, that there is no need to despair for if winter comes, spring cannot be far behind.

December Wines

Christmas knocks a huge hole in the cellar every year, especially now that it runs from December 20 into the New Year. See January's wine notes for suitably sombre reflexions on this aspect of our Saviour's Birth. One is tempted to serve less good wine to the younger generation, especially when they turn up with bright young friends professing a repugnance for the Christian religion, but there is always a risk that one or another – or all for that matter – might turn out to be Jews, at which point they would have one over a barrel. In fact there is no tradition for drinking good wine among the Jewish people, despite the fact that some of the best vineyards in France are or have been owned by Jewish families – Mouton, Lafite, Beychevelle spring to mind. Israeli wines are no good at all – at any rate I have never succeeded in finding one which was worth drinking – and one of the most disgusting beverages ever invented is served in New York Jewish households under the pretence that it is wine – an intensely sweet, intensely alcoholic preparation. They produce it on high days and holidays, but I honestly think I would prefer Somerset parsnip wine.

Be that as it may, Christmas is a time for producing the best wines, and that, where the reds are concerned, means grand old vintages. Old wine is by no means easy to buy, and is never cheap, although for those with the time to spend some interesting job lots can usually be found at Christie's regular wine auctions. The disadvantage of buying old wine at auction is that you can seldom taste it in advance, and you never know where it has been. Personally, I always like to know why it is being sold. If it has been sent in by a private seller – usually in a lot of eleven or ten bottles – it will probably be dud. However, if it is an entire cellar being sold, you may be very lucky indeed, and prices are noticeably lower than anywhere else in the wine trade, partly, no doubt, because the few wine merchants still dealing in older wines often buy their stocks at these auctions.

Otherwise Berry Bros. of St James's Street, London, still have large stocks of mature wine, including some of the cheapest and best old Burgundies available for those who like the heavy, malted taste of English-bottled Burgundy which most of us were brought up on. Avery's of Bristol also have a stupendous variety of old wines if you ask for their Special Listing, including, once again, some of the best old English-bottled Burgundies, although their prices have gone up since they bought a computer to look after that side of things. Another specialist in older vintages is Reid Wines of Hallatrow, near Bristol, with an ever-changing list which always has something of interest on it, and sometimes has amazing bargains. Further north I would recommend Adnams, of Southwold, whose wines may be tasted first in their excellent restaurant, called the Crown, and for conventional clarets and ports of the best vintages, ask Christopher Collins, of Bibendum, 113 Regents Park Road, N.W.1. for the Fine Wine Supplement to his ordinary list.

Those approaching the problem of finding good old wine for Christmas from a position of knowing little or nothing about it may care to arm themselves with the vintage charts and other advice available in Hugh Johnson's incomparable Pocket Wine Book, revised and updated for Mitchell Beazley annually and priced (1986) at £4.95 – putting it just in the 'D' range. But all the merchants I have mentioned are honest ones, and none will give bad advice.

It really does not matter whether you drink Grand Old Burgundy or Fine Old Claret with your turkey or goose, but if you drink neither I fear you may go to Hell. Italians of the thirteenth century knew little about wine, but if they had I feel sure Dante would have reserved a circle of Hell for those who are mean with their wine at Christmas. Mince pies are a bit of a problem, but young Sauternes goes incredibly well with Christmas pudding. In fact I would say it is about the best thing to drink young Sauternes with – far better than foie gras.

Stilton of the milder, creamier sort is a reasonable accompaniment for vintage port, but the best accompaniment in the world is nuts: hazelnuts, walnuts, brazil nuts, macadamia nuts, in fact any nut you can care to mention although salted peanuts and cashew nuts are least good and almonds a trifle unnecessary. If a man cannot drink vintage port at Christmas when on earth can he drink it? It is also particularly delicious with Christmas cake. One of the pleasantest and most sensible ways of getting through the whole Christmas season is to spend it munching Christmas cake and sipping vintage port from the moment you get up until the moment you go to bed.

Funny things have been happening to the vintage port market recently – partly inspired, no doubt, by the wine investment fiends, since vintage port, unlike vintage Burgundy or claret, never really goes off, and passes its peak so gradually over a fifteen-year period that nobody notices. It is thus perfect for investment. The last classic year, to replace the 1963s, was 1977, although 1983 was far from contemptible. The 1963s are only coming up for drinking now (unlike the 1966s, which have been drinking happily for three or four years) but the price of them – anything up to £55 the bottle for Taylor's, £50 for Fonseca – is prohibitive. In fact the whole vintage port scene is now bedevilled by absurd prices. Even the 1977s, which will not be ready to drink for at least twelve years, are costing up to £20 a bottle, although the greatly inferior 1975s, which should still be procurable from most wine merchants for around £11–£14, may be drunk now.

But there is not much point in drinking inferior vintage port and, for those without large cellars, an active life expectancy of more than twenty-five years or a huge bank account, the only way to drink first-rate vintage port at reasonable prices (say £12–£16) is to concentrate on the single *quinta* wines produced by the great houses in years when the quality is good enough but there is not *enough* premium vintage grade wine to declare a vintage.

The best of these single quinta wines are Taylor's Quinta do Vargellas, Fonseca's Guimaraens and Graham's Quinta do Malvedos. Vargellas is the property which produces the best ingredient in Taylor's vintage port, noted for its taste of violets over the splendid nutty characteristic of the fruit. It is my settled opinion that some of these Vargellas wines, produced in "off-years" like 1965, 1967, 1969, 1972 and 1974 are better than any except the classic Taylor's vintage years of 1963 and 1970 (I have not tasted their 1977). They are also less than half the price and released only when they are ready for drinking. The Vargellas 1965 available from Berry Bros at £16.50 is quite simply a dream, as is the 1974, just released and drinking splendidly, although it will undoubtedly improve for years. It will sell at around £12–£14. I do not regard that as an excessive price to pay for a taste of Heaven. My theory, ingrained by years of subjection to feminine rule, that nobody should drink more than two glasses of vintage port for fear of becoming liverish, bad-tempered and stupid, was triumphantly disproved on a visit to the beautiful home of Vargellas, miles up the Douro Valley near the Spanish border. I found one could drink ten or twelve glasses with no ill effects whatever, although it is wise to avoid the *bagaceira* or slop brandy, made from skins, stalks and pips left over from the pressing.

Finally, a word about champagne. One hears hymns of praise to the cheap champagne sold by Sainsbury's and other chain stores, and it is true that controls are now strict enough to ensure that no bad champagne is made. At weddings there is no reason not to serve such wines – my own favourite is a brand called de Telmont, from Majestic Warehouses, chiefly because, like Krug, Bollinger and Ayala, it has a very high proportion of black grapes – pinot noir and pinot meunier – in it to add richness at the expense, perhaps, of a certain chardonnay bounce obtainable from the best blancs de blancs. But at Christmas one should really do better. The standard big companies, like Moët and Chandon, Mercier, Lanson, may be overpriced in relation to less

famous but equally respectable wines which spend less on advertising.
In this range I would recommend Henriot (obtainable from Stevens
Garnier, of Botley Works, North Hinksey Lane, Oxford) for the light,
lemony, chardonnay taste, Billecart Salmon (obtainable from Windrush Wines of Cirencester) for the balance and Ayala (obtainable
wherever you can find it) for the rich pinot taste. Among more
expensive and "prestige" labels I have already mentioned Krug and

Bollinger (whose R.D. 1975 is second only to the almost unprocurable Vielles Vignes blanc de noir) for the rich pinot taste, and Laurent Perrier's Cuvée Grand Siècle for the balance. I do not believe that any of the blancs de blancs prestige labels are really worth the extra money. Might as well add fizz to some Chablis.

Some may be appalled by the cost of these champagnes, and I agree that they are worth it only if one is feeling particularly festive and particularly rich. Christmas is also a time for brooding about the poor. A useful and worthy thing to do. I feel that the best equipment for that gloomy occupation is a glass of good vintage port and a slice of Christmas cake.